THE
ISLAND
THAT
WASN'T
THERE

Ruth Snowden was lucky enough to spend her early childhood in two rambling old houses in the country, crammed with books, hidden corners, mice and ghosts. She began writing poetry and stories when she was eight and has never stopped since. One of her three children, Manda, was a real tomboy and always wanted to be a pirate – Rosie's character is partly based on her.

Ruth lives by the sea in Cumbria with her human family and a black cat called Purdy.

THE
ISLAND
THAT
WASN'T
THERE

Ruth Snowden

PICCADILLY PRESS • LONDON

First published in Great Britain in 2008
by Piccadilly Press Ltd,
5 Castle Road, London NW1 8PR
www.piccadillypress.co.uk

Text copyright © Ruth Snowden, 2008

A catalogue record for this book is available from the British Library

ISBN: 978 1 85340 996 7 (paperback)

1 3 5 7 9 10 8 6 4 2

Printed and bound in Great Britain by CPI Bookmarque, Croydon

Mixed Sources
Product group from well-managed
forests and other controlled sources
www.fsc.org Cert no. TT-COC-002227
© 1996 Forest Stewardship Council

For Manda,
who always wanted to be a pirate

Chapter One

The Old Git Gang

The boys never wanted me to join the Harbour Gang, because I'm a girl – but there weren't enough people really to make it a gang with just the two of them.

In any case, I'm the only one who actually *lives* near the harbour, so I guess that made me OK. That and the fact my dad works on the fish quay, unloading the fishing boats.

It was Cal's idea that I was only an associate. He's the oldest and he's really tough. He's got big muscles on his arms that he can make rock-hard and he rubs gel in his hair so it's all spiky like a yellow bottle brush.

Cal said I had to do a really hard test to become a full member. Plum thought I should hang above the water from one of the stepladders that go down into Queen's Dock and count to a hundred. Typical. He wouldn't do that himself – he's far too much of a wimp! Plum's real name is Ryan, but he's always called Plum. He's tall and gangly like a scarecrow

1

and he's only six months older than me, though the way he goes on you'd think he was a lot more.

But Cal saved me because he's the boss and he said dangling from the steps was too dangerous and our mums would kill us. He said he'd think of something else for the test. I wished he'd hurry up, so I could join properly and be a full gang member like Plum and Cal.

We do all sorts of stuff in the gang – things like fishing or swimming, or tree-climbing. Sometimes it's rock-pooling or beachcombing and sometimes it's pirate stuff. I like being Anne Bonny – she was a fearsome female pirate who terrorised the Caribbean.

Anyway – this particular Friday evening we were doing spying. We were spying on the Old Gits.

'Maybe we'll finally find out where they've stashed their treasure,' said Plum, 'and then we'll do a dawn raid.'

There were three of them, the Old Gits. I didn't think we should call them that, but Cal did, so I shut up. I didn't want the boys to leave me out.

'The Old Git Gang,' sniggered Cal. And we ducked down behind the harbour wall as the Old Gits tottered up to their meeting place.

'Shhh . . .' said Plum, 'they'll hear you.' But he sniggered too, and went red in the face. He thought it was a laugh. It was a good sort of joke, because we're the Harbour Gang, and there are three of us too.

The first Old Git to arrive was Old Plum. He's Plum's great-grandad. I asked Plum once why they were all called

Plum – him and his dad, and his grandad and so on.

'I don't know,' he said. 'There's just always been a Plum.'

Old Plum is about a hundred I think. He's tall and gangly with a long neck, just like Plum. But he's all wrinkled and dried-up like a kipper with being out in the salt air so much, working on the trawlers.

Pordy is wrinkled too, but he's short and fat with bow legs. He walks with a sideways lurch like a crab, and he always wears wellies with thick knitted socks rolled over the top. He used to work on the trawlers like Old Plum, and he still has a little boat with peeling blue paint called *Kittiwake* that he keeps in South Harbour.

And then there was Yan Eye. We were all scared of him. Even the boys. He only had one eye and it always seemed to look right at you like a shark about to eat you.

Yan Eye wore a cloth cap that was so greasy you couldn't tell what colour it had been when it was new. And he always wore a red scarf around his neck, whatever the weather.

Yan Eye was from away; he wasn't from our town. When he spoke, which wasn't often, his voice was soft with a strange lilt to it that wasn't like the way folk speak round here.

But nobody knew where he had come from. It was a mystery. He'd been around for ages. He used to work as a lumper on the dock, loading the fish on to wagons like my dad. And he had a small boat too – the *Hildaland* – that he kept neat and freshly painted.

The Old Git Gang always sit in the same place, on the wall by Queen's Dock. They almost seemed to have grown there – like seaweed or limpets. Any time you go down they are there – morning, noon or night. They even meet there if it's raining, or blowing a gale.

They never twigged on that we were listening to them. Our bit of wall jutted out at a right angle to their bit, so it was safe to get behind and spy on them. There was a pile of fishing nets on top, so we could look through the gaps and watch. But I was still scared they'd find us. If they did they might tell our mums we'd been spying and then we'd get our pocket money stopped or something.

'They're Old Gits,' said Cal, 'they won't. They're all deaf as posts.'

'Blind as bats too!' mocked Plum, peering through the fishing nets.

'Bats aren't blind,' I whispered. But Cal poked me, so I shut up again.

The Old Gits shouted at each other, because of the deafness. 'Grand day!' boomed Pordy. His voice is deep because he's got a big chest like a rum keg.

'Aye,' agreed Old Plum, in a cracked old whispery voice like a skeleton would have. He propped his stick against the wall and cleared his long throat. Then there was a silence. Yan Eye pulled his greasy cap down over his eye and said nothing. He hardly ever spoke.

They began to ramble on then and it soon got boring. It was like being trapped in the street when your mum meets her friend when you're out shopping. It was only good because we were hiding and they didn't know.

Even Cal began to fidget after a while, and we all stopped listening, but nobody wanted to get up and give us away. We didn't want the Old Gits to know we'd been spying.

'Wind's rising,' creaked Old Plum.

'Aye. It'll rain when the tide turns,' said Pordy. And Yan Eye nodded. That was all he had to do to be part of the conversation. He'd been in the Old Git Gang so long he didn't really need to speak.

My leg was going to sleep. I had my shin pressed up against the bucket we'd brought to collect covins in when the tide got a bit lower. I shifted it and rubbed a bit, and the bucket lurched and made a clang against the cobbles.

'Shhh!' hissed Cal. But it was too late. Yan Eye cocked his head on one side and homed in on us like a herring gull after fish and chips. *He* wasn't deaf.

'Rats behind that wall,' was all he said. But we knew he knew. He stood up slowly and came across. We all shrank down, trying not to be seen, but then his face was there, peering over the wall, so it was no good.

His one eye was green, like the smooth glass pebbles you find on the shore. It stared at us without blinking. And his empty socket seemed to stare too, like there was a hidden eye in it.

I screamed. I didn't mean to – it just burst out with the shock of it. Cal kicked me, right on the other shin, the one that wasn't already being pressed into the bucket.

'Shut up, Rosie!' he hissed. But it was too late. Old Plum's face appeared beside Yan Eye's. He shot out a wrinkled old

5

arm and caught Plum by the scruff of his neck and hauled him over the wall.

Plum kicked out and wriggled, but Old Plum hung on like a terrier. He's strong is Old Plum, even though he looks so dried-up that the wind might blow him away.

'Caught one!' he wheezed. And then he laughed. A horrid dried-up laugh like a dead goblin. He thought it was a huge joke. He dumped Plum down in front of the wall so he could get in more breath for the laughing.

Plum was red again. So red in fact that I began to wonder if that was why they were all called Plum in his family. He was bright red, like a ripe one. His sweatshirt was all rucked up, so he pulled it down and stood there staring at his trainers.

Cal and I came out too, because it was no good pretending to be still hidden. We all stood in a row in front of the Old Gits, feeling stupid.

'Were you listening behind there? Spying on us?' asked Pordy. It sounded really naff once he actually came out with it like that – we couldn't admit we *had* been spying and playing a silly game. I felt embarrassed and a bit scared. Pordy's hands looked big and rough like chimp hands and he had a big wide leather belt.

Plum just stood there and kept on staring at his feet. My voice had dried up in my throat and wouldn't come out. But Cal spoke. He always does, because he's the oldest.

'No,' he said, 'we were just planning where to go for covins.'

Pordy began to laugh like Old Plum. A deep rumbling

noise like distant thunder. Slow at first, then gradually faster, like his laugh was waking up after a long sleep.

But Yan Eye just stared at us without speaking, his one eye unwinking. He knew it was a lie, I could tell. I felt really scared then all of a sudden – like he might *actually* turn into a shark and swallow us up.

Chapter Two

The Dead House

Have you ever tasted covins? Some places they call them periwinkles. They have little round black shells and you find them in the rock pools when the tide goes out. They taste of grey rubber when you cook them.

Mum says we shouldn't eat them anyway because the sea isn't clean any more. But the Harbour Gang like to collect them sometimes, just for the fun of it. We usually put them back after.

Yan Eye stared at the covin bucket suspiciously with his eye. 'Took a lot of planning did it?' he said, in a doubting sort of way. Cal went a bit red and said nothing. Plum stayed scarlet.

In the end it was me that sorted it out. 'Actually we *were* listening,' I blurted out suddenly. 'We wanted to hear some of your old sea-faring yarns!' I just made this up on the spur of the moment – after all, the Old Gits probably *did* tell each other yarns when they sat on the harbour wall. Everyone looked at me, all surprised. Pordy began to chuckle again.

'That la'al lass is braver than you big lads!' he rumbled. Cal and Plum looked at each other shame-faced and I felt kind of proud but mad at the same time because I hate being called a la'al lass – a 'little girl'. I'm small with blond curly hair so people always think I'm cute. That only makes it worse.

Old Plum pulled a pipe out of his pocket. He sat down on the harbour wall and began to stuff it with ginger tobacco out of a leather pouch. Pordy sat down beside him, clearing his throat and spitting over the wall into the dock.

'Come and sit here, lass,' he said, lighting up a fag and patting a dry bit of wall next to him, 'I'll tell you a story *worth* listening to.'

I felt a bit scared still, but I didn't want to offend Pordy any more, so I went and sat down. Yan Eye sat down too, on the other side of Old Plum, so we were in a row – Yan Eye, Old Plum, Pordy and me, like a row of seagulls.

Cal and Plum were left standing there and shuffling their feet. They looked as if they still felt really stupid.

'See that building over there?' said Pordy, pointing to a stone shed on the far side of the harbour. 'They used to call that the Dead House.'

The shed was empty and boarded up, so we couldn't get in, but we'd always wondered what it was for. It had always given us the creeps a bit – it felt sad and deserted somehow.

Cal's eyes lit up and he forgot that he was feeling silly. 'Why?' he asked.

'That was where they put them. Corpses they dragged out the sea.'

Plum went a bit paler all of a sudden. He sat down, cross-legged, in front of Pordy and stared at him, waiting for him to go on. Cal sat down next to him. Plum's eyes went round, like gobstoppers, but he didn't speak.

'When I was a lad there was a big storm,' went on Pordy. 'Two men were drowned off a fishing boat out at sea. They never found one of them, but the other was washed up a week later, and they put him in the Dead House.'

There was a short silence. 'Did you *see*?' breathed Cal.

'Aye. Me and my mate Jack climbed up and looked in through the window.'

Plum gulped loudly. We all sat there not daring to breathe. It was really horrible, but we had to *know*. 'What was it like?' asked Plum in a pale, thin voice.

'Horrible! His face was all nibbled at by crabs, and he was all blue and —'

'That's enough!' butted in Old Plum suddenly. 'You'll have these nippers not sleeping at night, and then their mums'll be after us!'

Pordy chuckled and shut up, so we could tell we weren't going to find out any more about the Dead House. Typical of grown-ups, I thought crossly. They just get on to the interesting bits and then they decide you're not allowed to know that sort of stuff and they all gang up and go quiet.

Old Plum's pipe had gone out. He pulled the stuffing out with a penknife and knocked it against the wall. Then he began to fill it all over again, breathing slowly as he worked. When it was done he held it in his hand unlit and said slowly, 'I can tell you a tale too.'

'Go on then,' we all said. The Dead House thing was really scary, so we wanted more.

'See that bit of sand, right over there on West Beach?'

We all craned our necks to look. 'The bit along near the lighthouse you mean?' I asked.

'Aye. Under the wall there. That's Lucky Corner.'

'Why?' asked Plum. He'd found his proper voice again.

'There's a current flows up there when tide's in. Any money or stuff that gets chucked in the harbour tends to end up there. When we were lads we'd often go and look there, and find pennies in the sand.'

'Cool!' said Cal. 'We could try that.'

'Once I found a thin gold band, big enough to wear on your head,' said Old Plum. 'I took it home, but my mum made me throw it back in the sea.'

'Why?' said Plum. 'That was stupid! It was probably worth a fortune!'

'Mum said it was bad luck. Said she'd heard a story once when she was a little girl, about a gold band from the sea. It was cursed – if you put it on your head it made you long for gold and riches all the time and you could never get it off again unless . . .' He looked puzzled suddenly.

'Unless what?' I asked him impatiently. This was really interesting.

'You gave away every single thing that you owned, I think,'

said Old Plum slowly, staring out to sea as if he'd forgotten the answer and it might be out there somewhere.

'How did it come to be here?' asked Plum, drinking in the whole story like it was all true. I wasn't so sure myself – this might be one of the Old Git yarns . . .

'A mermaid could have lost it,' said Pordy, and he gave us a wink, to let us know he was teasing.

'Yeah *right*,' sneered Cal. He wasn't going to let them think he was childish enough to believe that.

'Stranger things've been seen lad, out yonder,' said Pordy, pointing out to sea and pretending to be offended. 'Never heard of the Disappearing Island?'

'What's that?' we all said together. It sounded magical.

'Just what it says – a disappearing island, all made of mist. Floats on the water like a great big cloud. Only appears every hundred years.'

We all popped our eyes and looked suitably impressed.

'Does anybody live there?' asked Plum, a bit nervously.

'Naybody knows lad,' said Old Plum, in a hollow voice. 'But they do say as folk 'ave *vanished*.'

'How do you mean?' I asked.

'If you row towards it – it moves away,' said Old Plum, raising his arm and moving it slowly to one side to show how the island moved. 'But if you *do* manage to get there . . .'

'You nivver come back!' chortled Pordy, almost choking on his fag.

'Aye,' spluttered Old Plum. 'Me Great-Uncle Tom managed to get there – *he* nivver came back!'

Pordy took his fag out and glared at Old Plum. 'Nay – weren't he lost off a trawler as well? Shouldn't make fun o' the dead.'

'You're both pulling our legs,' said Cal suddenly with a grin. Old Plum laughed and pretended to cuff the side of his head.

But I felt a weird shivery feeling. Like I somehow *knew* about the Disappearing Island, even though I'd never heard Dad mention it or anything.

Old Plum lit his pipe again, and stuffed it in his mouth. All this time Yan Eye said nothing. He just sat there with this odd little knowing look on his face, like he could have added more if he'd wanted to. We waited to see if he had a story too.

But it was Pordy who spoke up again. He pointed at Yan Eye. 'Ever wondered how he lost that eye?' he asked.

'No,' we all said politely, and shook our heads. But we did wonder of course. In fact we were bursting to know. We'd come up with loads of ideas of our own – all the kids had. Like he'd been shot at, or someone had attacked him with a knife. But nobody knew the truth . . .

'A shark took it!' shouted Pordy, with a sudden roar of laughter. 'Bit it out for a snack when he was swimming in the harbour!' He rocked and wheezed, amused by his own joke. But we didn't believe him.

'Nay,' said Old Plum, taking his pipe out of his mouth again. 'It wasn't a shark. It was a great giant squid. Fastened its tentacle on his face and sucked it out. Sllluurrrppp!'

We all laughed then, because it was so stupid. All except Yan Eye. He didn't laugh. I had to ask him then. Wanting to know made me brave.

'How did you lose it really, Mr Morgan?' I asked. That was his real name – you couldn't call him Yan Eye to his face, although all the children called him that behind his back.

He fixed me then with his one eye, and he looked very sad, as if he was looking at something far away. 'I lost it in a duel,' he said. And his voice was like winter.

I was amazed. I knew he was old – but not *that* old – to have had a *duel* – that was what people in *history* used to do!

There was a silence then, because you could tell by the chill in Yan Eye's voice that his eye was not all that he had lost in the duel. I felt sorry for him all of a sudden, looking at his old brown face with its one eye. Why was his face so sad? I wondered. What else had he lost . . . or who?

Chapter Three

A Storm for Midsummer

It's supposed to be hot in June. Flaming June they call it, meaning hot like a furnace. But Friday night, after school, it went really cold. Then there was a storm.

Mum sent our Alex round to the chip shop because she was too tired to cook after she finished her shift at Tesco's. I was sitting in the front window, watching along the harbour side for him coming back, because I was really hungry after being out all day. That was when I noticed the clouds beginning to bank up, low out over the sea.

Some of the cloud seemed to be forming into a separate lump that looked almost like an island floating on the sea. I pretended it was the Disappearing Island and imagined sailing there in a tall pirate ship.

But my magical island soon disappeared behind a great wall of grey fog, and the wind began to rattle the masts of the boats in the harbour. I love that sound, the clink, clink of the rigging against the masts. It sends me to sleep at night, like a special harbour song.

That night it was different though. The sky gradually went dark, then almost black, and the clinking of the boats grew restless like a warning. Then their rigging began to make a low, moaning storm sound that folk say is the voices of drowned sailors, crying on the wind – but I know that's just a scary story.

By the time Alex got back with the chips, a few big wet drops of rain had begun to splash on to the front-room window.

'Storm coming,' said Dad, glancing out at the sky over his chip paper. 'Pass the vinegar, Rosie.' He was watching the news, eating like a mechanical shovel, with his eyes glued to the telly. He always reminds me of a frog, our dad – he's short and squat and when he swallows food he really enjoys he kind of presses his eyes down into his head and gulps the way frogs do.

Alex burped and wiped his hands down his trouser legs under the table. Mum saw him do it. 'Right – that's it,' she said. 'Next pair of school trousers I wash you can iron yourself.'

Alex gave her a look, but he knew she meant it. He burped again, to show he didn't care. Mum burped too, much louder. It was a competition suddenly, but Dad won. He did a great long one like a drain, and Alex and I got the giggles so much we couldn't stop and I snorted tea down my nose all over my jumper.

Mum snapped then. 'What am I – a flipping washing android? Get that jumper off and up those stairs, young lady!' She was pretending to be mad, but I knew she wasn't really because the corners of her mouth kept turning up.

I shoved the jumper in the wash basket by the boiler and went upstairs to my room. By now there were angry white waves lashing all over Queen's Dock, and further out I could see big waves beginning to spray up over the end of West Pier where the lighthouse was.

I didn't mind. I like it when there are big waves because I can pretend I'm out at sea in a pirate ship. It sounds dead realistic, with the wind howling and moaning and the waves crashing.

But I didn't feel so swashbuckling when the first flash of lightning came just as I was getting into bed. I nearly jumped out of my skin! I leaped into bed and pulled the covers up tight around my neck. I always get scared in thunderstorms. It's not very brave and pirate-like I know, but I can't help it.

Spider Sam was scared too. He's a small, silky, red monkey with a cheeky little face and long thin arms and legs with Velcro on, so you can hang him up on things.

I hung him from the metal rail at the head of my bed and looked at his cheerful grinning face. 'Don't worry, Spider Sam,' I told him, 'we'll stay in port until the storm passes. And when we set sail you can be the powder monkey.' That's the boy who brings gunpowder to the cannons on board ship.

Spider Sam went on grinning – that's all he *can* do, because his mouth is stitched on. 'Aye aye, Cap'n,' I made him say in a squeaky voice. He was still scared.

We were both really glad when Mum came in to say good-night.

'Do you want a night light?' she asked. I nodded, so she went to get the oil burner – the one with twisted tree roots and branches round the place where you put the candle. It seems like you're looking into an enchanted wood when it's all lit up.

Mum put lavender oil in the top of the burner to help me sleep, and I could soon smell it in the room. But some-how my eyes wouldn't close. They just stayed open all by themselves, like they were jammed open with matchsticks.

As I lay there I began to worry about the test for joining the Harbour Gang properly. What was it going to be? Cal still hadn't said. It could be something to do with spiders . . . or dead jellyfish . . . I burrowed tighter under my quilt, listening to the storm and remembering the last time Plum really got up my nose.

'Girls can't be pirates!' he'd said scornfully.

'Yes they can! What about Anne Bonny?'

'Who's she anyway? You're always yarping on about her.'

'She was an Irish pirate,' I said, trying to sound all knowledgeable, 'in about seventeen hundred and some-thing. There's Mary Read too!'

Plum had frowned. He couldn't say anything to this – he could tell I knew my stuff. Cal backed me up. 'It's true.

They dressed as men and went to sea – I read about them in a topic book at school.'

'Yes,' I'd gone on, encouraged by Cal, 'and there's Alvilda – she was a Goth from Sweden, and Ching Shih . . .'

'Ching She, tee hee,' Plum had mocked, pathetically. He always gets all girly and feeble when he knows he's losing. I'd ignored him.

'She was in charge of eighty thousand pirates!'

Both the boys gaped at me. They couldn't beat *that*.

I smiled to myself under the bedclothes. I knew it was going to be even better when I was a full member, because then I could shut Plum up more easily.

I was still thinking about the test when the thunder and lightning began to die away. In fact, I'd only really counted three more crashes before it seemed to be over. But the wind went on, louder and louder, wilder and wilder, until I had to get out of bed and go to look.

Huge waves were crashing in by now, so high that they almost reached the top of the lighthouse. The light was still flashing, but it seemed like a candle out there in the blackness, almost blotted out by the angry dark of the sky.

I hoped there were no boats out at sea, and with a shudder I thought suddenly of the Dead House. The drowned sailor floated there in my mind's eye, all pale and wet on his stone slab.

Pulling the curtains tight shut against the howling storm, I ran back to bed and dived right down under the quilt. But I never shouted for Mum. I didn't want to get the Old Git

Gang into trouble. I'd never heard all those interesting yarns before and I didn't want to spoil our chances of hearing more. It made me feel more like a real pirate. The Old Gits were our friends now, even Yan Eye – sort of.

Chapter Four

Flotsam and Jetsam

Next day was Saturday. Plum came round in the morning on his bike and knocked on our door just as we were having breakfast. 'Emergency meeting,' he said, showing me a glimpse of his pirate scarf under his denim jacket.

That's our secret sign – wearing a pirate scarf round your neck. Mine's one with a red and orange pattern like flames. Plum's is black with skulls on and I'm dead jealous of it.

'Ten o'clock, usual place. Cal's orders.' He didn't say where, so Alex wouldn't know. We didn't want a gang of Big Boys coming.

But I knew where. Our meeting place is out on Sugar Tongue, by the statue of the boy looking out to sea with a spyglass. There's a mouse in his pocket if you look carefully, and there's even little carved bats hung up underneath where he sits if you know where to look.

After breakfast I made an excuse and dashed off out. I

made sure nobody was following and then I ran right along Sugar Tongue. I scrunched in under the statue on the seaward side, looking up at the bats and waiting for the boys. I didn't want to be seen by anyone else who would give us away. The wind had gone completely now. It was still cloudy, but really warm and the water was dead calm.

Cal gave me a real fright, sneaking up from the far side and going 'Boo!' all of a sudden. I jumped nearly out of my skin. But I didn't scream. We waited for Plum, and he soon turned up, red in the face again with running.

When Plum had got his breath Cal said, 'Right then. Beachcombing today, me hearties.'

'What for?' I asked.

'Flotsam and jetsam chucked out of boats and that,' said Cal. 'You'd better look hard, 'cos I've decided what your test is for joining the Gang.'

'What?' I said nervously. My voice wavered.

'You've got to find something on the beach that No Man Has Found Before.'

'What about woman?' I said.

'Eh?' said Cal.

'You said no man. What about woman?'

'Or woman then,' said Cal, a bit crossly. He didn't like having his leadership challenged.

'Cool!' said Plum excitedly. 'It'll have to be something really unusual. Treasure or something.'

'Treasure?' I said. I was excited too now.

'Or a keg of rum perhaps,' said Plum hopefully. 'We

could roll it up the beach for the Old Git Gang.'

'Get them rollicking drunk!' shouted Cal. 'So's they'll tell us more about the Dead House!'

I wasn't so sure about the last bit. But I followed the boys anyway. They ran off down Sugar Tongue towards West Beach, yelling like a couple of banshees.

But I didn't run. I walked slowly because I was worrying. How on earth was I going to find anything on the shore that No Man Has Found Before? It would be really impossible. My heart sank as I realised I was probably never going to be a full member of the gang.

We'd had a good look in Lucky Corner after what Old Plum had said. There were no gold bands lying around though. There were bottles and cans, lumps of driftwood, shells and plastic bags, all in tangled heaps. Cal found a big white fish crate, but it had a hole bashed in the side so it was no good. Plum found a black wellington boot.

'P'raps it's Pordy's,' he said. 'P'raps a shark ate the rest of him.'

'Don't get sharks that size round here,' said Cal.

'You do! My dad told me!'

'He was having you on!'

'Was not!'

'Was!'

'Was not!'

Plum lunged at Cal. Cal was standing below him on a pile of slippery, stinky seaweed, so it sent him sprawling, even though he's a head taller than Plum. I watched while they writhed and rolled about, having a fight.

'Your mums'll kill you!' I said. They were getting all seaweed tangled in their clothes, and Cal had a big streak of beach tar down his cheek. They stood up, panting and grinning, enjoying it. Cal swiped at Plum and they both went down again.

Meanwhile I got bored because fights are a boy thing. So I started untangling a mermaid's purse from some mangled old orange fishing net. It was a whole one and I wanted it to keep. It was a black, crackly pouch, with long twisty springs at each end.

They aren't really mermaids' purses of course. My teacher told me that. They're really egg cases from a fish. The springy things hold them on to seaweed. But it was fun pretending.

'Look!' shouted Plum suddenly, pointing down the beach. I think Cal was beginning to win, so he was desperately looking for something to distract him. We looked.

'Cool!' said Cal. 'There really *is* a keg of rum.' Something small and dark was bobbing in the waves at the edge of the sea. He set off down the shingle at a run, wanting to get there first.

It *was* a keg. A small wooden one, just like the ones in the wine merchant's in town. But when Cal picked it up it was really light and he realised it must be empty. A dark trickle of water came out of a small hole in the bottom.

'No good,' said Cal disappointedly. He chucked it back

into the water with a big splash and got sea all up the legs of his jeans. Plum seized his chance and shoved Cal from behind, so he staggered deeper in and got wet up to his knees.

For a moment Cal looked like a thunder cloud. I had to think really quick, before a *real* fight broke out. I knew that Plum would lose. He'd curl up in a tight ball on the shingle, trying not to cry, while Cal lost his temper and thumped him. He's OK is Cal, but sometimes he forgets how big he is.

'Wait!' I shouted hurriedly. 'We can still use it!'

The boys both looked at me. 'How?' said Cal doubtfully.

'We could . . . I know – we could play a trick on the Old Git Gang!'

Cal forgot to be mad at Plum. His temper never lasts long. 'How?' he said again, looking quite interested.

The keg was beginning to drift away from the shore as I spoke. 'Pretend we think it's full. But tell them we couldn't quite reach it. They'll have to row out to it in *Kittiwake*!'

'Hey yeah!' said Plum, grinning cunningly. 'We might get a ride.'

'OK then,' agreed Cal. He got out of the sea and wrung his jeans legs out, but they were still sodden. He didn't care though. This was going to be a smart laugh.

The Old Git Gang were sat in a row in their usual place. At first they didn't believe us about the rum keg, but I put on my innocent-blond-curls look. 'It's true, honest,' I said.

Strictly speaking this wasn't a lie, because there *was* a rum keg. We just didn't mention it was empty.

Pordy got up first. He liked rum a lot. 'Can't hurt to have a look, eh lads?' He got off the wall and began his crab-walking towards West Beach. Old Plum followed, grumbling and leaning on his stick.

But Yan Eye didn't get up. He pushed his greasy cap to the back of his head and watched the other two lumbering off. 'Daft pair!' he said, and carried on sitting there like his backside was glued to the quayside wall.

We felt a bit uncomfortable, him staring at us with his one eye. So we just left him and ran after Old Plum and Pordy. When we reached them we could see that the keg had disappointingly washed back up again, and was lying on the shingle.

Pordy staggered down the beach and picked it up. He shook it hopefully, but all he got was another trickle of sour sea water. Old Plum struggled down more slowly. He moved like a puppet with dangly arms and legs that wouldn't move where he wanted them to.

When he got there Pordy pulled a sour face. 'Empty!' he said. They both looked dead disappointed, like when Mum says you can go to the cinema but Dad gets in from work too late.

I felt a bit guilty, watching them walk back along the quayside. They looked tired and grey, like two tatty old gulls with their feathers moulting. It didn't seem as funny as I thought it would.

The boys must have felt the same really, though they didn't say. They pretended it was dead funny for a bit. 'Did you see Old Plum's face!' laughed Plum, sitting on the dry shingle and pulling the legs off a dead starfish. I wished he wouldn't, even though it was dead and dried-up.

'Aye,' laughed Cal, 'and Pordy must've thought he was in for a real good night!' But the laugh he did sounded a bit forced, and he and Plum soon wandered off, leaving me on the shingle. The beachcombing was over and the sky had gone grey again out over the sea.

I stayed down there a bit by myself, worrying about what Cal had said about the Harbour Gang test. I had to find something really unusual. A mermaid's purse didn't count – they were often washed up on the shore.

Maybe an unusual stone? Or I could cheat by just giving Cal *any* old stone and saying he couldn't prove whether anyone had found it before or not.

Somehow I didn't think Cal would fall for that one. So I sat down and began sifting through the stones, looking for a really strange one. But I couldn't find one that I thought would do, so I began chucking them into the water.

After a bit I found a piece of wood and tossed that in the water, so I had a target to aim at. I got into a drowsy sort of rhythm, with the grey waves and the splosh, splosh of the pebbles.

It was then I heard the noise behind me, up near the top of the beach. It sounded like somebody crying, only different somehow. Odd like – so it made the hairs go up on the back of my neck. I always thought that was just in stories, but my hair really *did* it, *whoosh*, in a shivery wave.

I looked all up and down the shore, but there was nobody there except me. The odd sound went on – a sort of thin wailing, like a gull makes far out over the water.

I stood up and walked along a bit, trying to find exactly where it came from. Then I realised there was an extra-big bank of seaweed, piled up in a long line near the harbour wall at the end of the beach. There must be somebody crying behind it.

It was quite steep – the waves had piled it all in a stinky, slithery mass. My feet squished into it as I scrambled up, like treading in old porridge. Or dead men's brains, I thought horridly, remembering the Dead House again.

The crying noise stopped as I was scrabbling up, as if the person had heard me and didn't want me to know they were there. It wasn't until I got right to the top that I saw her. And even then I didn't see her for a moment because her hair was the same green as the seaweed, so she blended in.

Chapter Five

Anemone

Her skin was greenish too. A sort of pale blue-green, like the aquamarine in Mum's engagement ring. And it looked kind of slimy, like a fish. She looked really ill, I thought.

She heard me scrabbling up the seaweed pile and turned her head to look at me. Half of her was buried, under a mass of twisted seaweed and bits of old rope, so I could only see to her waist. But she looked about my size, perhaps just a little bigger, so I guessed she was a bit older than me.

I nearly screamed when I saw her eyes, but I was so scared the scream got stuck in my throat like a cork. They were huge and very dark, like fish eyes, or some sort of weird insect thing. The silver-grey light from the clouds reflected in her wide-open pupils.

She smiled then, sort of, and began to speak. Her lips were thin, and her teeth, when I saw them gleaming white, were pointed – *sharp*-looking. But her voice was quite ordinary.

'Thank goodness,' she said, rather unexpectedly, 'can you help me get out of this lot?' She pointed to the seaweed that was tangled all round her legs. I hesitated for a moment – I was still wondering if she was some sort of giant insect . . . or an alien maybe? I shuddered when I thought of touching that pale fishy skin.

Mum had always taught me not to stare, and I knew that it wasn't some people's fault if they looked different. So I blinked and took a deep breath.

'Sure. Does it hurt?' I asked, beginning to feel sorry for her.

'No. I just can't move. It all got twisted round and round when the waves were thrashing me about.'

I couldn't understand quite what she meant. Had she been swimming in that big storm or what? If so she was a prat and she deserved to have been drowned. But I didn't say that. Instead I just sort of chatted politely as I began to untwist her.

'My name's Rosie,' I said.

'I'm Anemone,' she replied.

'Anemone? Like sea anemone?' I thought it was a strange name.

'No. Just Anemone.' She looked puzzled.

'How old are you?' I asked, changing the subject. She must be new to the area, and if she was younger than me, maybe I'd ask her to join the gang so I wouldn't be the youngest any more. Or the only girl.

'Six hundred and forty-one at the next full moon,' she said. Calmly, as if it was perfectly normal. I stared at her. Was she a nutter or what? She was obviously lying, but I still felt she'd got one up on me somehow. I felt myself go red, so I bent my head down. I was having to struggle with a particularly long strand of seaweed anyway. It was the thick, brown, strappy sort that grows right down by the low tideline.

I yanked it off at last and then began untwisting some hairy old blue rope. Anemone was wriggling her legs underneath, trying to help. She sat up and began yanking at some more seaweed.

All of a sudden a big lump of weed came away, and I could see her legs underneath. She had weird tights on. Sort of fishnet ones made of gleaming pearly stuff. There again, I thought, not fish *net*, so much as fish *scale*.

I stared for a moment, forgetting it was rude. 'What's wrong?' asked Anemone, pulling a long strand of green weed out of her hair. It was exactly the same colour, so it looked as if she was actually pulling her hair out.

'Your tights,' I said, 'I've never seen any like that. They're really cool,' I added hastily.

'Tights? What are tights?'

I pointed. 'On your legs. Your stocking things.'

She looked really blank. Her wide black pupils stared into me, swallowing me like dark holes in the sea. 'Legs?' she said, with a slight shudder. 'I don't have *legs*, you idiot.'

'Whh?' I mumbled. My mouth closed up. There were

no words I could think of to say. I felt as if I'd been really rude. Perhaps she was disabled or something. But hang on . . . I was sure I'd felt her legs thrashing about under the seaweed.

Anemone looked exasperated. 'For goodness' sake. You look as if you've swallowed an eel!' She rolled her eyes right up into her head, and turned her thin lips down into a pout. 'Mermaids don't have *legs*. We have *tails*!'

I must have looked dead gobsmacked. My mouth just hung open, so I looked like a fish too.

'That's my *skin*,' she said sarcastically. 'Not *tights*. Whatever they are.'

My mouth came back to life. 'No kidding,' I said slowly. I felt as if my brain wasn't working properly. 'You're a *mermaid*!'

'Sure. What's wrong with that?'

'So mermaids are *real*?'

Anemone pulled the last of the seaweed away from her tail. It lay there on the pebbles, gleaming like a huge fish. I couldn't take my eyes off it.

''Course we're real,' she said scornfully. 'Do I *look* as if I'm not?'

'Well no, but . . .'

'Huh!' she snapped suddenly. 'You humans are so pathetic! You think you're the only ones on the planet!'

I didn't know what to say to that, so I kept quiet for a moment. Anemone gazed out to sea and suddenly she looked really sad. A pale, misty, white tear like a pearl rolled

32

down her cheek and lay shimmering on the seaweed pile. It looked solid.

'I want to go home,' she sobbed suddenly, bending her head and covering her eyes with her hands. I noticed then for the first time that there were delicate webs of skin between her fingers – like a duck's feet, for paddling through the water.

I put my arm around her. She wasn't cold and slimy at all like I'd thought. She felt warm and soft. 'Where do you live?' I asked her, just like you'd ask a kid who was lost in town.

'Over there, under the waves.' She pointed vaguely out to sea and the light shone through the web of skin between her finger and thumb. 'Many miles away . . . it's a long swim and . . .'

Her voice trailed off. Secretly I thought she was a bit of a wimp. Six hundred and forty-one and she couldn't find her own way home. But I didn't say so.

'Don't you know the way?' I asked.

'Of course I do,' she said faintly. 'But normally I would ride.'

'Ride?'

'A sea horse. Don't you know *anything*?'

'So where *is* your sea horse?' I asked, ignoring how rude she was being.

'How should I know?' she snapped, suddenly looking angry. 'He bolted when the lightning flash came and I was thrown off his back. That's the only reason I ended up tangled up in all this seaweed in *this* dump.'

'In any case,' she added, 'it's far too dangerous for me to try and swim back home alone. It's the Finfolk. They're back . . .' Her voice trailed off again. She looked even paler, like she felt sick or something.

'Who're the Finfolk?' I asked. I didn't like the sound of them much.

But Anemone seemed to be rambling, like people do on TV when they're in shock or something. 'I don't want to be a Finwife . . .' she said, her voice wavering. 'A sad, miserable being . . .'

'What do you mean? What's a Finwife?' I asked. None of this was making any sense at all. Who were the Finfolk? Where were they *back* from?

'The wife of a Finman of course! Finmen are cursed – they have no girl children of their own so they have to marry mermaids – or humans.'

'Humans?' I didn't like the sound of this either.

'Yes. When they force you to marry them you grow sad after seven years, really depressed after fourteen . . . and then . . . you become a Finwife! The most miserable being imaginable!' Anemone broke down and began to sob uncontrollably.

It was then, as she sat there with her webbed hands covering her eyes, that I first noticed the bracelet on her wrist. It was made of tiny fragments of shell and coloured stones, joined together on a thread as fine as a hair. A covin shell was fastened at each end to make a clasp.

I had never seen such a beautiful delicate thing before. How could anyone possibly have made it? I reached out my hand to touch it. It felt cool and somehow powerful – as if some unseen magic flowed from it.

But I soon pushed this strange new feeling to the back of my mind. I was a pirate, wasn't I? Pirates had to be tough and rough and fierce, not interested in girly bracelets. And Anemone needed my help right now to get her home without the Finfolk kidnapping her out in the open sea.

'Don't worry,' I said gruffly, giving her a squeeze around her shoulders. 'I'll help you get home safe.' Hopefully the Old Gits would help with one of their boats. But would they believe me – especially after the rum keg incident?

Chapter Six

A Tear of Pearl

I covered Anemone's tail with some of the seaweed to stop her drying out. She was getting shivery and looked even paler green than she had before.

'Will you be OK while I go for help?' I asked anxiously.

'Yes . . . but hurry. I don't like being out of the water for long.' Her spiky teeth were beginning to chatter together. Another pearl tear slid down her cheek and landed on the seaweed. It didn't soak away – it just lay there looking solid like the other one had.

Curiously I poked at the tear, and it rolled a little way, so I picked it up with my finger and thumb. It *was* solid, just like a real pearl. It lay in the palm of my hand, glowing with a faint pink sheen. I slipped it into the small top pocket of my jeans and stood up.

'I'll be as quick as I can,' I said. 'I know some people who've got a boat.'

'Please hurry,' she said again. Her voice was fainter, like the wind sighing over the water.

It was on my way along the harbour that I suddenly realised I'd done it! Cal would have to accept finding a *mermaid* as something really unusual. I decided to find the boys first and tell them. Luckily they hadn't got very far.

They were sitting on the edge of Queen's Dock, dangling their legs over the water and watching a cormorant diving for fish. I saw it going down with a slick movement like oil and then bobbing up again further along.

I dashed to the boys all out of breath like. Then I had to double up for a minute to get rid of a stitch in my side before I could blurt the words out.

'Quick! Where's the Old Git Gang? I need their help!' I panted at last.

'Why?' asked Cal. 'They've just gone off for dinner, I think.'

I glanced along the harbour towards The Anchor pub. They always went there for a pie and a pint at dinner time. They must have already gone inside, because they weren't still tottering along the dock.

'Come on then. We'll have to get them,' I yelled, and set off again at a run. I could only go sort of limpingly because my air was still used up. The boys came too. They could tell there was something urgent going on.

'What's up?' shouted Cal, jogging alongside me easily. His legs were a foot longer and he hadn't just run all the way back from the beach like I had. I hadn't enough breath to explain anything properly.

'Mermaid,' I gasped. 'Found a mermaid.'

Cal stopped running and burst out laughing, grabbing my shoulder and forcing me to stop too. 'A *what?*'

'Mermaid,' I said again, faintly. My voice tailed off. Cal didn't believe me. And now I'd actually said the word *mermaid* out loud I had to admit it sounded pretty naff.

'A mermaid. *Right,*' said Cal.

'Yeah, yeah,' joined in Plum, who had been running just behind, 'she found a *mermaid*. She's a girl pirate and she found a *mermaid*.' He said 'mermaid' in a wet, feeble little voice. He can be right nasty can Plum, specially when he thinks he's better than you. Any time he can he'll sort of gang up with Cal to try and make you look small.

They both stood there and looked at me, with these stupid grins on their faces. I could have hit them both. Or burst into tears. But I thought of poor Anemone, lying there on the shore shivering and getting paler and paler.

'OK,' I yelled angrily, 'don't believe me then! I don't care about your stupid old Harbour Gang any more!' And then I just wheeled around and ran off towards The Anchor, leaving them both stood there staring after me. I couldn't have cared less if the ground had opened up and swallowed them right there.

I burst in the door of The Anchor and ran right up to the bar. I knew kids weren't allowed in unless you were with your mum and dad, buying you a meal. But I didn't care about that either.

Pordy was there, perched up on a bar stool, supping a pint. Next to him was Old Plum, propped against the bar like a mouldy old scarecrow. His pint was just being drawn from the pump. I watched it frothing into the glass.

Pordy put down his pint with a loud sucking sigh, and wiped the foam off his lips with the sleeve of his grubby, navy blue jersey. He stared at me with his mouth open. Old Plum turned round and stared too, like I was some sort of alien.

The whole pub went all quiet and I felt very conspicuous all of a sudden. There seemed to be Pordies and Plums sitting at every table. Lots of old men, with pints on the tables in front of them, or stopped in mid-air halfway to their lips in surprise. And *all* of them were looking at me.

I took a deep breath, tasting of fuggy pub air and spilled beer. Grabbing at Pordy's woolly sleeve I blurted out, 'Mr Wilson, Mr Wilson, you've got to come quick!' But Pordy just looked at me. So did Old Plum. So did all the other Pordy and Old Plum clones sitting round the tables. Even the barman stared at me curiously.

'And why would that be, lass?' asked Pordy slowly, cocking his head on one side and raising a tangled eyebrow.

'There's a . . . there's someone stranded, down on the shore.'

'Who's that then?' asked Old Plum, with a look of mild interest. 'Someone stuck in a rum keg, eh?' He and Pordy smiled cracked old grins, enjoying the joke, waiting for me to say more. They had me trapped, like a worm on a hook.

'No. No . . .' I looked around me wildly. Faded old eyes were focussed on me from all sides. A door opened and I could see it was Yan Eye, just emerging from the Gents. He would come and stare at me too, with his one green eye.

Suddenly I felt scared. All these old men, and not one of them would believe me, any more than Cal and Plum had. 'She's a mermaid,' I shouted desperately, 'and she can't get home!' I just didn't know what else to say. It sounded *really* stupid, even to me.

There was a ghastly silence that seemed to go on for ever. Nobody spoke. The barman put another pint down on the bar with a clunk. Suddenly I remembered the pearly tear in my pocket.

'Look!' I yelled. 'I can prove it! This is one of her tears!' I fished it out and held it up, glowing with its strange pink light in the dark fustiness of the pub. It looked beautiful, like it was the only alive thing there.

Well that did it. The entire pub just erupted. Pordy laughed so much he had to double up and nearly fell off his bar stool. Old Plum wavered about and knocked his stick over on to the floor with a clatter. And all the other Pordies and Plums roared with laughter too. It was ghastly.

At last Pordy drew breath and managed to stutter, 'That's a good 'un lass. Even better than the rum keg!' before he set off chuckling again. Tears streamed down his cheeks and he had to clutch his sides to hold himself together.

Old Plum was as red as a beetroot, so red I was scared

he'd burst and it would be all my fault. 'If you think I'm missing me pie for a flipping mermaid,' he gulped, 'you must be daft!' That set all the other old men off again. The whole pub just rocked and roared.

But Yan Eye had come up silently to stand beside me. He took the tear gently out of my hand and held it up to the light. And the look in his one eye was sad. Sad and sort of long ago, like autumn.

'I'll come with you, lass,' he said, handing the tear back to me.

Chapter Seven

Everything Goes Wrong

It wasn't what I'd meant to happen at all. I meant Pordy to come and help, or Old Plum. Not Yan Eye. I felt dead scared as I followed him down the quayside towards West Beach.

I kept thinking about his eye. His one eye boring into me, seeing that I was telling fibs. Even though I wasn't, because Anemone was real. But how could you tell that to a grown-up?

The other thing was that I wanted the boys to come. That had all gone wrong too. I'd found the most unusual thing *ever* on the beach and they just didn't believe me. Now I'd never be a full member of the Harbour Gang.

Yan Eye walked fast and I had to do a half-run to keep up. When we got to the beach he stopped suddenly and turned round. 'Where is she, lass?' he asked. I felt more scared than ever. What if I'd imagined Anemone?

But I knew I hadn't, so I pointed to the long line of lumped-up seaweed at the far side of the beach under the harbour wall. 'She's there, behind the seaweed,' I said. Yan Eye said nothing. He just strode off across the stones with this grim look on his face.

He probably wants to prove I'm lying, I thought. But I followed anyway, stumbling over the stones. I couldn't just leave Anemone there alone, drying up like a stranded fish, dying on the shore.

I fell over because the stones were all loose and slithery, and by the time I caught up again Yan Eye was standing on top of the seaweed mound looking down the other side.

I scrabbled up too, clinging on to the weed and trying not to think about the Dead House and Yan Eye's eye socket all empty and sewn up like an Egyptian mummy. He was just standing there, looking down, when I got myself upright again.

'Where?' he said in his strange lilting voice, pronouncing the 'wh' sound very clearly and drawing it out like a gust of gentle wind. Yan Eye never used a sentence if one word would do. I pointed to where I'd left Anemone.

'There . . .' I began. But my voice trailed off, because Anemone had gone. There was just seaweed, starting to smell in the sun, and lots of little beach hoppers jumping about. They're mini beasts that live on rotting stuff on the shore. I stared at them. Had they eaten Anemone? Already?

Yan Eye stood there saying nothing. I stood there too, because I didn't know what to say. Then I opened my

43

mouth and a small tickly voice came out. 'She's gone,' I said. And then there was a long horrid silence, like when the teacher discovers someone hasn't done their work and is about to tell them off.

But Yan Eye didn't tell me off. He just turned to look at me. The missing-eye side of his face drooped sadly and his one eye stared at me, unwinking green like cold, deep water.

It was like the rum keg all over again. He didn't look angry – more sort of disappointed, like he'd really *wanted* there to be a mermaid on the shore.

He pouted his mouth up like a fish and shrugged his thin old man's shoulders. And then he just turned round without saying another word, and walked off slowly, *scrunch, scrunch* across the stones, leaving me alone.

I felt terrible then. *Nobody* believed me. The boys thought I was making it up just to get into the gang. All the Pordies and Old Plums in the pub thought I was a sweet, silly little girl with golden hair, seeing things. And now even Yan Eye thought I was fibbing.

I slumped down on top of the seaweed pile, not even caring if I got slime all over my jeans. What on earth was I going to do? Nobody would ever believe me again. I'd never be a full member of the gang. And what *had* happened to poor Anemone?

Tears began rolling down my own face now, just like they had on Anemone's. Only mine weren't pearls, just hot little wet splashes. They soaked into my T-shirt and dripped into the seaweed.

After about five minutes though I stood up and dried my face angrily on my jacket sleeve. This is no good, I thought, pirates don't cry – Anne Bonny wouldn't. I found a stick and poked about among the seaweed a bit, but there was no sign of Anemone. Nasty flies began to buzz up and whirl around my head.

Sadly I wandered off along the beach and began to make my way homewards. I was so wrapped up in my sadness, walking along with my head down, that I forgot I had to walk past the Old Git Gang's place until I was nearly there.

They were all there, sitting in their row of three, staring at me. And worse than that, the boys were there as well, grinning all over their faces.

Old Plum took his pipe out of his mouth and knocked the ash out against the harbour wall. A grin was spreading all across his face too. I was going to be laughed at again and I felt a sinking feeling in my stomach.

'Well, well,' said Old Plum, 'look who's been washed up on the shore now!'

'Aye,' said Pordy, 'the little mermaid!' He sat there with his short legs wide apart, hands resting on his knees. And he began his rumbly laugh again, deep in his chest.

Cal turned round and spat expertly into the harbour water. I watched the spit go down and land on a slick of oil that floated near the wall. The slick was full of bits of twig and stuff, all floating in a mess.

'Not found anything then?' said Cal, slightly mockingly. 'Anything *real* that is,' he added slowly. He pulled a Super

Soaker out of his jacket and aimed a jet of water at the spitty oil slick.

'Any sea serpents?' asked Plum, beginning to go red. 'Or female pirates' wooden legs?' He exploded then in a giggling frenzy. Like a big girl's blouse, as Dad would say. Cal sniggered too and then looked at me enquiringly, waiting for me to speak.

Suddenly I found this weird, wild rage inside me. I was all pent up what with worrying about Anemone and feeling shut out of the gang.

'Shut up!' I yelled. 'Shut up the lot of you!' And then I dashed off, head down again so they wouldn't see the tears that were welling up once more and starting to pour down my face.

I ran all the way home. Mum was in the kitchen doing the ironing when I burst in the back door. She was doing the collar of one of Alex's school shirts and she was all red in the face. She gave me a worried look when she saw the tears.

'What's up, Rosie?' she asked. But I didn't answer. I just rushed through the kitchen and up the stairs to my room and banged the door shut.

Chapter Eight
Pieces of Eight

The tears just made me mad with myself and I wiped them away on my pirate scarf. I sat on my bed gulping and hiccuping. Then I went over to look out of the window, out across the sea.

Where did Anemone live? I wondered. Still, it was no good wondering now – she'd vanished, hadn't she? A small nagging doubt slithered into my head. Had I made her up? Just because I wanted to join the Harbour Gang so much?

But if I'd made her up I must be really clever. I'd made up the webbed fingers, the green hair ... the fishnet skin ... and the tear of pearl! Where was it? I rummaged in my jeans pocket. It was still there.

The day had turned very dull now, with low clouds banking in from the west out over the sea. But the tear still glowed faintly pink, almost as if it was lit from inside.

It *was* real then. And if the tear was real, then Anemone

must be too. She might be still around somewhere and still needing my help. And there I was just sitting crying like a great sissy!

Spider Sam was hanging from the head of the bed. 'What shall I do, Spider Sam?' I asked, pulling him down so his Velcro arms made a soft tearing noise. He stared at me helpfully but he still said nothing of course.

The rest of that day was miserable. I just went on worrying about Anemone. And that night the wind moaned and howled sadly, like it was a lost mermaid crying. I just couldn't get her out of my mind.

In the morning when I drew my curtains the sky was blue. But everything felt dull and hopeless. I went down to breakfast with Spider Sam and propped him up against the cereal packet while I ate. He smiled in his friendly way, as if he was about to say something.

We went back up to my room then and lay on my bed, imagining I was in a hammock at sea. I lay there for ages, pretending I could feel the deck rolling under me. I could hear gulls mewing right outside my bedroom window, so that helped.

But really I was fed up. I wanted to go out and play. But I couldn't go out and look for the boys after what I'd said about the Harbour Gang, could I? I tried to read a new pirate book I'd got for my birthday for a while, but I couldn't get my brain to focus on it at all. So then I tried drawing a picture of a mermaid with coloured gel pens.

It was hopeless – it looked like a stupid, soppy girl dressed up. Just like my friend Melissa from school, in fact. She goes to tap-dancing and she's always dressing up in frilly outfits and winning stupid cups and things. She thinks she's fantastic. Big deal.

I screwed the mermaid picture up into a cross, tight ball and chucked it in the bin. Then I just sat staring dismally out to sea. Poor Anemone, I thought. She must think I don't care. But then suddenly, in a great rush, I knew what to do.

I picked Spider Sam up and told him excitedly: 'I'll find Anemone all on my own if I can't be in the Harbour Gang! I'll pretend to be Anne Bonny – a female pirate would never want a man to be the boss anyway, would she! I'll show the lot of them – stupid boys and stupid Old Gits!'

I got off the bed and went across to look out of the window at the harbour. It was still fine and sunny. A good day to go off on a lone adventure.

Spider Sam was watching me, lying on the bed all long and thin. He wanted to come too. So I picked him up and said to him, 'You can be a monkey that I found in the Amazon forest. Pirates often have pet monkeys from far off lands.'

But I hid him in my jeans pocket – I didn't want anyone seeing him and thinking I still played with baby stuff. And then – I don't know why I did it – I checked that the tear of pearl was there too. I suppose it was like a reminder that Anemone was real.

Suddenly I could smell food and I realised I was very hungry, so I dashed downstairs two at a time to see if lunch was ready.

Mum just stood and stared at me when I burst into the kitchen, almost as if I was really Anne Bonny. She gave me that *How come you always look such a scruff* look. She's in league with Auntie Lyn who has dyed blond, permed hair and always wears these really high heels. They're always buying me soppy pink stuff like hair scrunchies in the hope I'll turn into a girly girl. Some hope!

By the time I'd had lunch I felt even better. Just let anybody get in my way, I thought fiercely.

It felt really cool being Anne Bonny as I swaggered along the harbour towards West Beach. I felt bigger, stronger somehow, and I didn't care that I was going on my own now to rescue Anemone.

Only two of the Old Gits were in their place – Old Plum and Pordy. I steered clear of them because I didn't want any more stupid comments. Yan Eye seemed to be missing. There was no sign of Cal and Plum anywhere either, but I didn't care.

When I got down on to the shore there was still loads of stuff from the storm lying about. The tide had been in and gone out again several times by then, but it was a low tide, so it hadn't touched the stuff higher up the shore.

But there was still no sign of Anemone anywhere, even when I climbed the seaweed bank and looked down where she'd been lying. So while I thought what to do next I pretended there'd been a wreck, and I was Anne Bonny salvaging stuff from it.

I pulled Spider Sam out of my pocket and fastened him

through one of the belt loops on my jeans now that there was no one around to see. He could help me with the search.

'The Wreck of the *Helvetia*,' I said, drawing an imaginary sword and sweeping it through the air.

We'd had a postcard from Auntie Mags last summer with a picture of the place the *Helvetia* was wrecked. It was in South Wales really, but that didn't matter – I liked the sound of the ship's name.

The real *Helvetia* had been carrying wood as a cargo, but that was too boring, so I decided on chests full of gold. Pieces of eight. I picked up an old plastic bucket that had lost its handle and began to fill it with small, flat pebbles that would do.

It was quite absorbing, finding pebbles of exactly the right shape and size, and I slowly wandered further up the beach without noticing. I was so busy looking that I'd forgotten all about Anemone until I heard the cry.

It was the same cry as before, like a seagull floating on the wind, but so far off and thin this time that I thought I'd imagined it. I stopped and listened. No – there it was again. And it was coming from behind the seaweed bank, just like before.

I dropped the bucket full of gold and dashed up the beach. I struggled up the seaweed pile again and peered over the top. There was *still* nobody there.

Slumping down on the smelly pile I sank my head in my hands. Was I losing the plot or what? But then a thin salty voice said quite distinctly, 'Is that you, Rosie? I've just woken up. Thank Neptune you came back!'

I sat up with a jerk and looked more closely. There was still nobody there. But as I stared I began to make out a faint, wavery outline. It was like trying to see one of those 3D pictures. The more I looked the less I could see. But it was Anemone all right.

She'd gone so pale and see-through that you could see the beach through her. Pebbles and seaweed and stuff. It was almost as if she was made of the shore. But her outline was quite clear, once you really knew where it was.

'Anemone! So you *are* there! Why didn't you say before?'

'That man,' she wavered, 'the man with one eye . . . '

Yan Eye! Of course – Anemone had been scared of him, just like I was. A visible shudder went rippling through her edges. I felt a shiver too for some reason, right down my spine. But I pretended I wasn't bothered.

'Oh, he's just Yan Eye,' I said airily. 'He does look a bit scary, doesn't he?'

But Anemone was too weak to reply. She just let out a small hissing sigh, like the way the sea sounds at the tail end of a small wave on shingle. She needed help, and fast. What was I going to do?

'I'm drying up,' she said faintly. 'My tail – it feels all stiff.' And sure enough, when I looked at it I could see her tail was starting to look all dried up – the way a fish does when you leave it out of water too long.

I stood up and looked around me desperately. But I

couldn't think of any way to shift Anemone down to the water. She was a bit bigger than me and besides – how was I going to get her home? I didn't have a boat and nobody would help me.

'What can we do?' I wailed. 'I can't carry you. Can you slither?'

'I . . . I don't think so. I'm too weak . . .' said Anemone in a voice that was like a wisp of wind. She was a bit more visible though – I couldn't see the beach through her any more. I wondered why and I was about to ask her, but just then a soft voice spoke right behind me. I nearly jumped out of my skin.

'I'll carry you,' it said. I whirled around. It was Yan Eye. He hadn't been there a moment before I swear – in any case, I'd have heard him scrunching up the beach even if I hadn't seen him. It was like he came out of thin air.

Poor Anemone bared her fading teeth in a kind of snarl, and put her webbed hands across her eyes. 'No no,' she shrieked, 'I won't go with *you*! A stupid old man like *you* could never fight off the Finfolk!'

I wondered why she didn't just vanish again like she had before. In fact, she was growing steadily more visible by the moment. Maybe Yan Eye had taken her by surprise too, I thought – so she didn't have time to fade.

Yan Eye ignored her wailing. He picked her up as tenderly as a baby and wrapped her in his tweedy old jacket. He stood there in his shirt sleeves, holding her close to him. 'Don't fret, lassie,' he said in his soft lilting voice,

'I'll see you home all right.'

Anemone didn't react for a moment – I guess she was kind of in shock. Then she began to struggle like a fish and he nearly dropped her. She was screaming thinly and she sank her sharp little teeth into his thumb.

But Yan Eye muttered a curse under his breath and wrapped his jacket more closely around her so she was pinned helplessly. Then, before I could stop him, he set off really fast down the beach with Anemone in his arms.

And all I could do was run after him. He had his boat, the *Hildaland*, pulled up at the edge of the sea. How on earth had that got there? It hadn't been there before, when I was gathering pieces of eight in my bucket.

Yan Eye waded right in, getting his trouser legs wet, but he didn't seem to mind. He unwrapped Anemone and bent down to hold her under the water for a moment. But he held her firmly so she couldn't wriggle away.

When he lifted her out of the water again I gasped in amazement. Her skin was shining – a soft pale green like spring leaves, and her tail was sparkling and shimmering like a fish that has just been lifted from the sea.

Yan Eye wrapped her up in his jacket again, all dripping wet, and then lifted her into the stern of the boat and covered her with an old grey blanket. She wriggled a bit, but she didn't seem to make any attempt to climb out. Yan Eye began to push the *Hildaland* off the shingle into the water.

'Wait!' I shouted. 'I'm coming too!' I wasn't going to

abandon Anemone now. Yan Eye turned and looked at me with his one eye. For a moment I was really scared of him again. Then he silently held out his hand to help me into the boat.

Chapter Nine

On to the Open Sea

I know I shouldn't have gone. Thing is, I never really thought how it could be dangerous or anything. Mum had warned me not to go anywhere with strangers. But Yan Eye wasn't a stranger, was he?

I was so worried about Anemone getting home safely that I just climbed in without thinking. It wasn't until Yan Eye had pushed the boat right out and started to row that I really began to realise what was going on. And by then it was too late.

And it was then that something *really* horrid happened. Yan Eye bent down to pick up the oars and the red scarf he always wore around his neck slipped for a moment. He soon shoved it back into place, but not until I'd seen.

Under the scarf he had *glistening gills*.

Like a *fish*.

I tried to scream somewhere deep inside me, but nothing

happened. I was so scared that I couldn't say anything, or even make the faintest squeak of sound.

I glanced over to see if Anemone had noticed, but she wasn't looking – in fact she was almost totally covered by the grey blanket. Only a long strand of seaweedy hair was showing. Just as well, I thought. I don't want her freaking out again.

Then, as Yan Eye grasped the oars and began to row I noticed something else. A thin thread of green stuff trickling down his thumb.

Could it be *blood*? I wondered, with another lurching shock. *Green blood* trickling from his thumb, where Anemone had bitten him? He saw me looking and hastily wiped it away on his jacket sleeve.

It *couldn't* be. Could it? Green blood? And he had gills! Only fish have gills, I thought. My brain was screaming, *This is not possible. None of this is possible.* What *was* he? Some kind of freak?

Nobody said anything. It was unreal. We rowed out of the harbour and round the end of the West Pier past the lighthouse. Then we were in the open sea. At first this was exciting and I almost forgot that I was in a boat with a mermaid and a – a weird, inhuman *fish thing*. I'd never been this far out on the open sea before.

It looked really odd the way the land just came to an end in a straight line all the way along the coast. I could just make out our house in the distance, with the little wooden flower boxes underneath the downstairs windows and the green front door.

Up on the hill was the church and above that my school. I could see the fence around the schoolyard, but no children playing because it was the weekend.

The sea was quite calm, but even so little waves began to lift the *Hildaland* up and down in a gentle rocking movement. Gradually my tummy began to feel a little bit odd, but I ignored it because I was being a pirate again so as not to have to think about Yan Eye's gills. I was Anne Bonny – I was used to being at sea, wasn't I?

Being Anne Bonny helped and I kind of forgot Yan Eye was a fish thing and blotted it out because it couldn't possibly be real. My brain was protecting me and telling me I must have imagined it.

Yan Eye just sat there rowing the boat and staring back towards the harbour. He looked so ordinary. Like the usual Old Git who sat on the harbour wall. I ignored the green blood.

I wished I could have a go with the oars, but I daren't say anything. The land gradually got farther and farther away and suddenly I was scared again. Everything I knew was getting smaller and smaller in the distance. Mum, Dad, our house on the quay, my school . . . and even Alex. I was even missing Alex!

The sick feeling in my stomach grew bigger. And I was getting cold. A chilly wind was starting to whip the waves up bigger as we got farther from the shore, and I had no coat on. Just a T-shirt and my jeans.

I tried to shrink down into the bottom of the boat below the sides to keep the wind off me. Being a pirate was beginning to seem less fun than I'd thought it would be. How did pirates keep warm, I wondered?

Grog. That's it. They had grog – or a tot of rum. That's why they were always rollicking drunk. But Yan Eye didn't seem to have any rum aboard. There was just a smelly tangle of old fishing net and stuff in the bottom of the boat.

All this while Yan Eye just kept on rowing and not speaking. All you could hear was the splash, splash of the oars in the water and seagulls keening in the distance. Yan Eye never seemed to get tired, even though he was an old man. The *Hildaland* skimmed across the water like a tern, much faster than seemed possible. And the oars didn't even seem to dip into the water very often.

I watched Yan Eye curiously. His face was stern and dark, but I realised suddenly that he might have been handsome once. When he was young and before he'd lost his eye.

There was a moan then, from the mound under the grey blanket on the bench beside me. Anemone! I pushed the blanket to one side until I could see her face.

She was still quite visible and that pale, faintly luminous green. It seemed the right colour for her, as if being on the sea was doing her good.

She looked beautiful, with her dark alien eyes reflecting the sky. But she looked scared too, and I realised she was even more worried about Yan Eye taking us out to sea than I was.

'Don't worry,' I whispered. 'We'll get you home. We won't let the Finmen get you.' But I wasn't too sure really. Could an old man like Yan Eye row that far? And what if the Finmen came?

Yan Eye's scarf was wrapped tightly around his neck as it normally was, so I couldn't see the gills any more. But I knew that they were there, impossibly and horribly – under the wool.

He isn't human, said a voice inside my head all of a sudden. *Is he a Finman? He's got gills – and Anemone's dead scared of him* . . . And, like the sick feeling, I tried to push that thought down too. I focussed on being Anne Bonny again, to make myself feel brave and fierce, so that I could defend myself and Anemone if I had to.

Who are you kidding? said the tiresome voice in my head. *He's a great big man and you're just a little girl.* Then I realised, with a horrible swoop like a great big rushing wave, what I had done.

I'd got myself and Anemone into real danger, out on the open sea with a man – no, a *thing* – who might as well be a stranger. He could do *anything* to us.

But there was no escape now. We were well out to sea and the *Hildaland* just kept on skimming over the water, almost as if it was being pulled along by some invisible force.

We travelled on for ages. Anemone was silent, huddled under her blanket. I could just see her eyes peeping out, wide and dark as wells. I began to wonder how long this would go on and where Anemone actually *lived?* Was it a place – like an island or something? Or was it totally under the water, and invisible? If so, then how would Yan Eye know when we got there?

Just then Anemone struggled her top half out of the blanket and sat up. She pointed a long, thin, green arm out to sea behind Yan Eye.

'Look,' she said, 'over there!' And we both looked, Yan Eye and me. He had his back to where we were going because he was rowing of course, so he had to twist his head round.

Away on the horizon was a strange block of mist. Just floating there all on its own at the place where the blue sky met the blue sea. Like the mist I'd pretended was the Disappearing Island – only bigger, and in a more definite shape.

Yan Eye drew in his breath with a sudden gasp, and then slowly let it go in a long drawn-out hiss.

'What is it, Mr Morgan?' I dared to ask. Curiosity had given me my voice back. Anyway, Yan Eye hadn't murdered me yet, so maybe he was safe after all.

He turned his face towards me and gave me that empty look with his one eye. It was a moment before he spoke and the silence seemed to hang in the air like a big wave waiting to crash on to the shore.

'Hildaland,' he said in his soft, lilting voice. 'That's Hildaland.' And his voice had a strange longing in it, like somebody mentioning the name of someone they had loved long ago who was now dead.

Anemone seemed to stare at Yan Eye when he said that

and to shrink right down under her blanket again. I was puzzled. Wasn't his boat called *Hildaland?* How could that low mist bank be Hildaland too?

'What do you mean?' I said, forgetting to be scared of him.

'The summer isle of the Finfolk,' he said. And he turned his bleak face again to stare out across the choppy water to where the weird mist was floating. It was just like a great big white cloud, sitting on the water.

I felt all shivery and scared all of a sudden. There'd never been an island like that out there before. It hadn't even been there *five minutes* ago, I was sure!

Could this island *move around?* And how could a weird cloud like that be an island anyway? Suddenly I remembered the Old Gits telling us about the Disappearing Island. *You nivver come back,* Pordy had said.

I felt colder than ever then, all down my back. And, once more, I began to wonder who Yan Eye really was again. How did he know about the Finfolk? He was just Mr Morgan, the Old Git, wasn't he? Or was he a merman or something, like Anemone? Had I *really* seen gills on his neck, and green blood trickling from his finger?

As I was staring at the peculiar white cloud I noticed something else. Tiny black dots were coming out of the edge of it. And they were moving towards us across the water.

It was at that point that Anemone went totally crazy.

Chapter Ten

Captive!

I've never heard anything like it. She started screaming like a banshee in this horrible high-pitched voice so I had to cover my ears. She was thrashing and wriggling too, trying to heave herself up to get out over the edge of the boat.

Yan Eye sprang into action. He yelled at Anemone, 'Finmen! Get *down*!' and he kind of pinned her down with one leg, awkwardly stretching it across the boat. With the other leg he tried to steady himself, bracing against the other side of the boat.

He looked really worried. He began to row incredibly fast, away from the mist island. He was really putting his back into it, plunging the oars in and out of the water so fast I was practically knocked over backwards.

But it was no use. The black dots were gaining on us, fast. One moment they were just distant black dots, then before you would have had time to blow a boatswain's whistle, I began to make out what they really were.

They were little round boats. Four of them. Each boat had someone in it, standing upright and rowing along with a single oar. All of them wore sinister grey cloaks, with great loose hoods that hung over their faces, so they looked like ghosts.

To and fro went the oars in a strange, coordinated rhythm like they were doing some sort of weird dance. And the little boats moved across the surface of the sea so fast that you just wouldn't believe it.

Although the white cloud that was Hildaland was away on the horizon the little boats appeared to be already halfway across the distance between us. Then they were getting nearer . . . and nearer . . . until I began to see the faces of the people who were rowing.

I wished I hadn't. I reached for Anemone's cool, damp hand and grabbed it under the warm wool of the grey blanket. I felt her squeeze my hand back and we clung on to each other like limpets.

They were men with long faces, solemn and grey-green like the sea, and lined with sorrow. They reminded me of Yan Eye, even though he wasn't the same colour.

Their eyes, when they got close enough for us to see, were pale and watery, like looking into cold rock pools. And their hands . . . their horrid hands were webbed and fishy-looking, with blue veins and white at the knuckles where each man grasped his long wooden oar.

Suddenly the first boat bumped into us. It gave me such a shock that I nearly fell into the bottom of the boat. Anemone began to whimper helplessly – a terrible sound, like a child crying in the night for its mother.

I must admit I didn't blame her. I felt sick with fear myself. Yan Eye was no help – he stopped rowing and just sat there like he'd been drugged, gazing straight in front of him without blinking. He didn't even *try* to row away any more. What was he doing? Was he betraying us – delivering us to these horrible Finmen?

A second boat bumped us with a sickening lurch, and then a third. And then I felt cold, fishy hands grasp me from behind and a web of damp, froggy skin closed across my eyes. I was dragged backwards and pulled painfully over the side of the boat.

Finmen, I thought, with a freezing-cold shudder, as I felt myself being dumped into the bottom of one of the little round boats. Almost immediately a horrible blindfold of wet seaweed was slapped across my eyes and tied tightly around my head. It stank, and a wet trickle of sea water ran down the back of my neck.

Then my hands and feet were bound roughly together too, with coarse scratchy rope. And I could feel a bruise coming up on my forehead where it had hit the side of the *Hildaland* as I was hauled out.

I wanted to shout at the Finman who'd dragged me into his boat, or stick my imaginary Anne Bonny sword in him – how dare he take me captive? Just wait till I tell our dad,

I thought fiercely. But Dad wasn't there to help me. He was somewhere across the cold sea, back home.

I was worried about Spider Sam too. I'd forgotten all about him dangling from my belt when I was being Anne Bonny on the shore. What if he'd fallen off somewhere?

It was terrible. I couldn't reach down to feel if Spider Sam was still there or not, because my hands were tied together. I wriggled and squirmed, but it was no use.

Great tears oozed up into my eyes under the seaweed blindfold. But I clung on to them, didn't let them seep out. They wouldn't make me cry. I was a pirate, wasn't I? Pirates don't cry.

I couldn't see what happened next, but I could tell by the swish of the long oar and the up and down movement of the boat that we were moving again. The Finman's feet must have been near my nose and they stank of rotting fish.

It seemed like only a few moments until there was another bump. This time it must have been on shore somewhere, because the boat lurched as the Finman climbed out. Then I felt him pull it up over shingle that scrunched along the bottom with a noise of wet pebbles.

Next I was lifted out of the boat. For a moment, I was pressed against the Finman's rough wool cloak. It smelled of rotting seaweed and damp things in caves I'd rather not think about. I found it hard to breathe and my heart hammered, thinking of that terrifying, sad face so close to my own.

But he laid me down quite gently on the shingle and I was

surprised to find that it was lovely and warm. I burrowed my cold arms and legs into it gratefully. It was bliss after the cold wind out at sea.

And there was a gorgeous new smell wafting into my nostrils – what on earth was it? It took me a moment to realise that it was quite distinctly the smell of ripe apricots. I love fresh apricots, and I'd know that smell anywhere.

I heard another boat scrunch up on to the shingle, and then the Finman from my boat spoke. His voice was not what I'd expected at all. I thought it would be harsh and grating like the barman at The Anchor.

But it was quiet and delicate, like the wind sighing gently over the water and I realised then all of a sudden, with a ghastly sinking feeling, where Yan Eye's soft lilt had come from. He *was* a Finman!

Another Finman replied, but I couldn't understand what they were saying. It wasn't English, or any other language I recognised. I heard two more little boats pull up on to the shingle, before my seaweed blindfold was removed so I could see where we had come to.

We were on a beautiful beach, like nothing I had ever seen before. It was made of tiny pebbles that looked like coloured glass. All the colours of the rainbow were there – yellow and orange and blue and bright sparkling red.

It was like being in a dream – the colours were so bright and clear I just couldn't believe my eyes! I sank my hands into the shingle and raised them again, letting the amazing pebbles run through my fingers like jewels that glinted in the sun. It was so beautiful! How could it be the home of such sad and ugly people?

Sounds came and went, and I could vaguely hear Finmen's voices. But none of it mattered. I felt calm and happy. Is it a weird dream? I wondered.

I didn't care any more. I just went on sifting the pebbles. And I forgot all about Anemone, and Yan Eye and everything. I even forgot to worry about Spider Sam.

Chapter Eleven

Hildaland

At last, after what seemed like hours, I looked up dozily from the pebbles. Warm sunshine was soaking into my neck. The sea was calm and blue like the sky above. It all felt so peaceful.

But just out to sea, only a little way away, was a thick white bank of fog that stretched right along the horizon. I realised then, finally, that I must be on the shore of the Disappearing Island – only now I knew its *real* name was Hildaland. I was sitting looking out to sea, on the *inside* of that strange white cloud that cloaked this mysterious, drifting island, hiding it from view.

The fog was so thick it looked like cotton wool, floating on the sea. I stared at it for ages and ages. It was pure white, so bright it seemed to dazzle my eyes and make my brain go fuzzy. It was like the hypnotic pebbles all over again, and I went off on another dream journey.

I seemed to drift in and out of the white, fluff wall of the cloud. My arms and legs felt heavy, and I could only move them slowly. Then I became fluff myself, floating on the warm breeze, like thistledown.

I don't know how long I drifted like that. It was almost like I didn't exist any more. I didn't seem to be able to think straight at all.

Part of me, the fierce pirate part, was struggling to try and make sense of what was going on. Was this really Hildaland? Why had I been brought here?

But being drifting fluff was soothing. I didn't really want to think about what was going on. It was too scary. Much too scary. Better just to drift, like a little summer cloud . . .

. . . All of a sudden there was a scrunching sound, like somebody walking on shingle and I came back to my normal body with a lurch.

Immediately a horrible thought flooded into my head. Anemone! Where was she? Had the Finmen taken her somewhere while I was dreaming on the pebbles? And Spider Sam! Where was he? How could I have forgotten about him all this time? My hand groped frantically for my leather belt and I looked down.

Spider Sam was gone. I twisted all around, looking for him, but he wasn't there any more. What if he was alone in the boat? Or worse still, he might have fallen into the water. I looked towards the sea in a huge panic.

The four Finmen were standing on the beach in front of me.

Yan Eye was standing with them and one of the finmen was untying a blindfold from around his eyes. For a moment the scarf around Yan Eye's neck slipped again and I glimpsed the horrid pinkish gills.

It made me feel sick. How could they be true? I rubbed my eyes, but Yan Eye had shoved the scarf back in place. He stared at me, with that lopsided far-away look, but he never spoke.

He never even tried to get away from the four Finmen. He just stood there, staring, and his face was sad, so sad it looked like winter trees all bare and leafless.

What was going on? Why was Yan Eye being so pathetic? Suddenly I wished again that Dad was here. He'd have laid straight into *anyone* that threatened us kids. But Dad was miles away across the sea. And Yan Eye never moved. He must have *wanted* us to be taken captive really, all along!

I looked around frantically, trying to see if there was anywhere I could run to if they untied my legs. But it was no use. I was surrounded by Finmen and I knew I wouldn't be able to run very fast across the pebbles.

One of the Finmen pulled the *Hildaland* up on to the shore. He had a short rope stretched from her across to his own little round boat. He must have dragged her along behind him as he rowed.

I still felt really weird, like I was in some kind of time-warp. I couldn't have been here very long after all – surely they would have pulled the boat up as soon as we arrived? Anemone *must* be here too!

But there was no sign of Anemone anywhere. I was just looking around and wondering where she had gone when my own Finman reached up and unfastened a buckle at the neck of his cloak. It was shaped like a dolphin and made of a metal that looked like silver.

He let his cloak fall down on to the shingle and then bundled it up into a rough ball and put it in his boat. Under the cloak he wore these really cool clothes – a sleeveless tunic and a short skirt of pale sea-green and gold that shone with a rainbow iridescence like butterfly wings.

On the front of the tunic was a circular design showing a silver dolphin against a dark green background. It looked like an emblem of some sort.

His bare arms and legs were the same strange luminous green that I'd seen on Anemone's skin. Then I had another shock. Hanging down each side of the Finman's body were huge draped green things that I thought at first were a second, finer sort of cloak, worn under the rough woollen one.

It wasn't until he moved to pull his little boat a bit further up the shingle that I realised what they were. And a scream rose up and got stuck in my throat like a fish bone.

They were fins. They fanned out under his arm as he pulled the mooring rope. The sun shone right through them, like thin green paper. And then I realised that now he was no longer wearing his hood I could see horrible gills down the side of his neck, just like Yan Eye's.

I felt sick and scared right down into my legs. I watched the gills with a weird feeling of fascination. They were pink and glistening, and they moved faintly in and out as he breathed. I could imagine his breath, coming and going in little fish-smelling gasps.

That's odd, I thought. He looks like he's a fish, breathing underwater. I'd seen them doing it in the Seaworld Aquarium. But we're on land – aren't we? Suddenly I wasn't too sure any more. I felt faint, dizzy. Maybe we're underwater, I thought. But if so, how come I can breathe?

I backed away, scrabbling up the shingle. It must be a bad dream all this. I must wake up soon. Mermaids . . . men with fins . . . Old Gits with gills . . . I pinched my leg to make me wake up. But I didn't.

The Finman walked towards me. He untied my feet then and his fins moved and rippled gently, more like strange clingfilm than paper. The sun caught them in pretty rainbow colours.

My head felt swimmy trying to understand what was happening. I vaguely knew I should get up and run, but I just sat there, rubbing at my ankles where the itchy rope had been. Long red marks were coming up – he'd tied it a bit tighter than was necessary.

The Finman yanked me to my feet and half pushed me, half carried me up to the edge of the shingle, where there was soft grass, so short and so green it looked like plump cushions of moss. He let go suddenly and I slumped down again.

Another Finman brought Yan Eye up beside me, and then I was pulled to my feet. We were both pushed gently forward and a Finman with purple fins grunted softly and pointed along a rough track that led away from the shore.

He wanted us to start walking. But my legs were all wobbly, like they were made of cotton wool. Yan Eye didn't seem to be affected the same way – he was walking in his normal, long-legged, Old Git kind of way.

Where were we being taken? And where on earth was Anemone? She seemed to have vanished into thin air. Maybe she had done her going invisible trick again. Right at that moment I wished that *I* could do it too.

Chapter Twelve

Through the Dream Land

I tried to look back at the *Hildaland*, where the Finmen had pulled her up on to the shore, to see if I could tell where Anemone was. But the Finman with purple fins pushed me again and I had to start walking away.

As I moved forwards I twisted desperately around one more time to try and spot Spider Sam. There was no sign of him at all on the beach. Would he float if he fell into the sea? I imagined him swimming along, his long red arms working like paddles. But would his body get all waterlogged? Would he sink down slowly under the waves?

Purple Fins gave me another gentle shove, so I gave up looking for Anemone and Spider Sam and concentrated on walking. It was really hard to stay upright at all. I kept stumbling and trying to sink back down on to the ground and sleep.

At the same time my brain was screaming, *This isn't real.*

It's a dream and soon I'll wake up and be back in my own bed at home.

But I didn't wake up. The dream feeling went on. And things seemed all odd and sort of disjointed, like they always do in real dreams. If dreams can be real . . . Soon we were out of sight of the boats, stumbling away from the shore up the rough track.

We came to a field with cows – well, sort of cows. They were the usual black and white type – but they only had front legs. The back part of them tapered into black and white fishy tails.

They dragged themselves slowly along the ground like seals, using the two front legs and munching stuff that looked more like seaweed than grass. My head felt more swimmy than ever.

I still couldn't understand if I was on land or underwater. Why did the cows have weird fishy tails? Were they mer-cows?

I was feeling really scared too. The dreamy feeling I'd had on the beach was beginning to wear off but things still didn't seem normal. Was I sleepwalking or what? I tried to force myself to wake up properly, by pulling my own hair and pinching my arms. But we just carried on walking in that weird dream world, and the mer-cows went on munching the seaweed grass like they were normal cows.

One of the cows stopped munching. It raised its head and stared at me. It had the same huge black glassy eyes that Anemone had. I stopped stumbling along and just stared into them. It was like falling into a well.

But one of the Finmen barked something in his strange language and pushed me from behind so I staggered on again. The way still sloped gently uphill and soon we were passing a second field full of strange crop-like little flowers close to the ground.

I stared closely because I realised they were sea anemones. *They can't be,* thought the awake bit of me. *Sea-anemones don't grow in fields.* But there they were – a whole field, all full of them! They stretched away, right down to the edge of the water further along the shore from where the boats were, away to our left.

They were red. Their tiny tentacles swished and waved like they were underwater. Their redness sucked me in and swirled all through my brain. I stood stock-still and carried on gazing at them, swaying on my feet. But I was soon pushed along again by the Finmen. I felt like a helpless little ant being dragged along by bigger ants. Where were they taking us?

We left the fields and began to walk past little round houses, all made of cobbles. Each one had a small garden around it, fenced in by twisted stuff that looked like dead bits of coral reef.

If I'd been dreaming up until now, at this point I swooped into a nightmare. Terrifying images were swarming past my eyes.

There was a skinny woman working in one of the gardens, digging the sandy soil with a creamy white spade like a bone. She wore a dress and a rough shawl flung around her shoulders. But she was as thin as a skeleton and her skin was pale, like dead fish. And her face was awful. Her eyes were red and bloodshot-looking, and her mouth turned down in a miserable sneer.

Finwife. That's a Finwife! I thought. A ghastly shudder ran through my whole body, and I tore my eyes away.

Another image immediately swooped into view and was gone again: two little boys playing on the step of a cottage, with a *crab* on a long green lead. They were feeding it with scraps of something nasty. There was a reek of rotten fish.

Once again I was shoved roughly from behind. The Finmen didn't want me stopping to stare at their women and children. Purple Fins grunted something in the strange lilting language, and Green Fins laughed in reply.

I stole a look at Yan Eye to see if he'd got the joke too, but he was staring straight ahead as he walked. He didn't seem any more amused than he normally was. Which was not at all.

'Where are they taking us, Mr Morgan?' I asked him, though I didn't much want to know really. My voice echoed inside my own head and I thought I might be going to be sick.

'Up to the palace,' he replied, with a dark scowl on his face.

'The *palace*?' I hissed, surprised to think that this mysterious Disappearing Island could have a palace on it, and moreover that Yan Eye knew about it. He'd obviously been here before then. I wanted to ask him more but his scowl got blacker than ever and he just stared straight ahead without replying, so I shut up. I was struggling not to be sick anyway and it made me feel worse talking.

The dream-like images went on coming. More fields full of strange cattle and red anemones. Orchards of trees with impossibly bright blue fruit, smelling like apricots. So that was where the smell had come from!

Children were running everywhere and others weirdly moving through the air with fishy tails. This made me even more confused – how come some of them had legs and others had tails? And were the ones with tails moving through the air – or swimming?

I remembered then what Anemone had said: *They have to marry mermaids – or humans.* Perhaps the ones with tails were half mermaid? And the others – the ones with legs – I didn't want to go there. It was too scary to think about. What if I got trapped here until I was grown up? Would they make *me* into a Finwife?

Then we came to a town and walked along narrow cobbled streets where tall gloomy houses almost blocked out the light. All of a sudden we stopped, and I realised we were standing in front of the palace gates.

It wasn't at all like you would imagine a palace. There was no mighty gate with guardian dragons embossed on the door. No towering spires of gold or anything. Nothing that a pirate would want to find in fact.

The gates were made of driftwood. Just ordinary, dull driftwood all twisted and heaped up into a rough barrier. On either side were windows, made of a mosaic of glass pebbles from the beach, all stacked up with layers of green cement in between.

Then a great horn sounded and I came to my senses. The driftwood gates were swinging open.

Chapter Thirteen

The Fin King

Inside the palace it was disgusting. You wouldn't want to go there, trust me – it was really gross. There were only small windows for a start, so the whole place was dim and dismal. The stone floors were wet and green with slime. And worst of all, it stank of fish.

It was almost like being underwater in the harbour, round by the fish quay where they throw all the scraps for the gulls to eat. I wouldn't have been surprised to find I really was underwater.

My feet kept slipping on the wet floor because I was wearing my old trainers and the soles had nearly worn off. The Finmen were OK because their feet, which were enormous, were bare. They were like huge, pale green flippers going flap, flap, flap on the damp floor.

We went along several corridors that all looked the same. Then we passed through a huge wooden door. It had a fancy pattern on it, and when I looked closely I saw it was made of tiny barnacles, just like the ones that grow all over the rocks at the edge of the sea.

Then we were in a great big hall. There was a bit more light in there, coming in through green glass windows set high up in the walls. But you couldn't see out at all because the windows were too high above the ground.

Below the windows were huge tapestries almost covering the walls. They seemed to be made of dried seaweed and bits of old fishing rope and stuff – the kind of junk you'd find on the shore.

The pictures on the tapestries showed Finmen in hunting scenes. Only they weren't hunting stags and boars. They were hunting sharks and stingrays. And they were mounted on huge sea horses with long tails that coiled like snakes.

I noticed one of the tapestries seemed to have women on it. They must be Finwives I thought – but not like the miserable Finwives. They were happy and beautiful, with long golden hair. They were sitting at a vast table with some Finmen, having a feast. All kinds of seafood were heaped up in silver dishes, and salads of seaweed were mounded in great bowls.

Purple Fins grunted behind me and pushed me forwards again before I had time to take it all in. We walked right across the great hall, and then we came to a pair of big doors with patterns on.

This time the patterns were not made of barnacles. They were made of gold and silver, and mother-of-pearl, all inlaid into the wood. They were swirling patterns, like shoals of tiny fish.

As I looked at them they seemed to be actually swimming. Swirling and flashing, changing direction just as real shoals of fish do. I stared and stared and my head began to reel again.

Suddenly a new seaweed blindfold was slapped around my eyes from behind. It was totally unexpected and it felt just as horrid and slimy as before. I wanted to rip it off. Then there was a creaking noise as if the great wooden doors were opening, and I was shoved forwards rather roughly and nearly lost my balance.

I started to protest, but a voice I now recognised as Green Fins hissed in my ear: 'Silence in the Presence!' I didn't know what he meant, but it was frightening nevertheless. What presence? I listened carefully, trying to find out. Then I suddenly realised I'd *understood* what he said, even though I somehow knew he hadn't said it in English! Maybe the magic of the island was soaking into me, making me able to understand the language?

It went completely quiet then. But somehow I knew that there were people looking at me. You know that odd prickly feeling you get sometimes when you think you're alone and you feel like someone's watching you all of a sudden? It was like that. It was as if the silence had eyes.

Then a man's voice spoke out of the silence, and a stream of ice shivered up my back, right up to the top of my head. The voice was cold and hissing, like a snake. 'Unbind his eyes!' it commanded.

I guessed that must mean Yan Eye. There was a squishy flapping noise like Finmen moving to take his blindfold off. But mine stayed on.

'Why do you trespass in my waters, Human?' demanded the voice. There was a brief horrible silence. Yan Eye was obviously saying nothing as usual. Then at last he spoke, in a gravelly voice that sounded as if he was speaking with his jaw clamped shut in anger.

'Do you not know me, Haldor?' he said. That was all. What on earth did he mean? There was another ghastly silence. Somebody coughed across the other side of the room.

Then the voice spoke again – it sounded really angry too this time. 'How do you know my name, Mortal? Who are you – that you dare to speak the name of the Fin King?' it roared. 'Make yourself known!'

But Yan Eye said nothing more. I wished desperately that I could see what was going on. The voice laughed. A cruel, slow laugh, like water gurgling in an under-sea chamber. 'Lost your sense as well as your eye? Hah! Let's see if your child will speak!'

His child? Surely nobody could think that wrinkly Old Git, or Finman or whatever he was could be my *dad*? I nearly blurted this out, but I kept quiet, waiting to hear what Yan Eye would say.

But Yan Eye still kept silent. He didn't say anything to try and protect me. I wanted Dad again. Desperately. I took several deep breaths to make myself feel brave and tried to imagine I was Anne Bonny, standing there with my sword.

But it was impossible. I knew I was just me really. I had to cope with this on my own.

Then the voice started on me. It spoke more gently this time. 'And you, mortal child . . . Who are you, and why do you come to stand in front of my throne?'

To my horror I found my voice had gone all thin and wavery. 'I . . . I'm Rosie,' I said feebly. I bit my lip fiercely. I didn't sound very brave, did I? But it was really weird trying to talk to someone you couldn't even see. Especially when that someone was obviously a king. I cleared my throat.

'I'm standing here because your men brought me,' I went on. I tried to look fierce and stand tall – the way I'd seen Alex when he was about to get into a fight. But inside I was still all quaky.

'Yesss,' hissed the voice. 'I don't take kindly to trespassers.' It was a nasty damp, fishy voice. It sounded old and sad, like one of the Old Gits on a bad day. But there was something that reminded me of Yan Eye too – the same soft lilt was there somewhere.

'I'm sorry,' I said, 'I didn't know.' I wondered why Yan Eye wasn't sorting all this stuff out anyway – *he* was the grown-up.

'What treasure do you bring?' said the voice, with a nasty, greedy sort of feel to it.

'I . . .' My voice was wavery again. 'I didn't know I was supposed to.'

The Fin King began to laugh. It was a deep gurgling sound that sort of built up slowly, like a drain unblocking. It sounded as if he hadn't laughed for ages.

'The child amuses me,' he said at last. 'Unbind its eyes.'

That made me mad. Its eyes! I'm not an 'it', I thought fiercely. Then I felt one of the Finmen untie my seaweed blindfold and I found I was glaring straight into the eyes of the Fin King.

I forgot to be afraid because of being mad. I glared at him full on. That seemed to amuse him too and he began to laugh again. His shoulders began to shake first and then it spread to his whole body and he threw back his head and roared.

I was amazed. He wasn't hideous and slimy and old, like his voice had suggested. He was the most handsome man I had ever seen.

His hair was gold and curling. And I mean gold. It actually shone and caught the light like real gold. And around his head, exactly the same colour as his hair, I noticed a circle of pure gold, like a kind of thin crown.

His skin was the pale greenish colour of all the Finmen, but his face was sculptured, like a beautiful statue. And his eyes were green too – like sea-washed glass. Like Yan Eye's eye.

He had the Finman gills too, wafting gently in and out on the side of his neck. They made him look alien and scary at the same time as being handsome.

But then he stopped laughing and looked at me again and I felt that tide of cold wash over me like the sea in winter. He's sad, I thought, so sad he looks like his heart must be broken.

His mouth drooped down in an unhappy curve, and there

were little lines of sadness all around his beautiful green eyes. He stared at me, like I was expected to say something else. I felt myself turn red. I hate that, so I looked away.

There were Finmen all around me. I saw now for the first time that I was in a completely circular room. The walls were painted glaucous green, and a low bench covered in seaweed ran right round the perimeter of the room.

Seated on seaweed cushions were Finmen, each wearing a dreary grey cloak like the ones I'd seen Purple Fins and Green Fins wear out at sea. Their hoods were all pulled up, partly hiding their faces.

The floor was awash with salty-looking water, and each Finman dabbled his webbed toes in it. Not one of them spoke; in fact each Finman had a hand across his mouth like he wasn't *supposed* to speak. But they were *all* looking at me.

Yan Eye was standing beside me and in front of us was the throne of the Fin King. It was made of driftwood, with twisted legs and gnarled arms.

Then I noticed that to one side of the throne was a vast pile of treasure. There were shining silver goblets; boxes with gold spilling from their open wooden lids; ropes of gleaming pearls; twisted gold necklaces; rings with rubies the size of pigeons' eggs.

My mouth just fell open and I couldn't speak. Where on earth had all *that* stuff come from? And why was it just piled up in a great heap like a load of old rubbish – shouldn't it be in a strongroom or something? It must be worth an absolute fortune!

'Have a good look, child,' said the Fin King suddenly. 'None of it's worth a herring to me any more.' I looked at him again then because his voice sounded so sad. Slow and sad like someone whose birthday has been totally forgotten.

Suddenly I had an idea. Maybe I could cheer him up. It was probably silly, but I *did* have something I could offer him.

'Wait a minute,' I said, 'I *do* have a treasure!' I reached into my pocket and held up the tear of pearl for him to see. It lay there in the palm of my hand, glowing faintly pink in the greenish light.

I wasn't expecting him to take much notice of it really. After all, it was so tiny beside his huge pile of treasure.

Chapter Fourteen

Crawling in the Dark

What happened next nearly scared me out of my skin completely. The Fin King stood up in a great watery swoop and the draped fins on his arms opened in a fan of pure gold. He kind of hunched over me, like a greedy vulture.

I was hypnotised. Partly by terror and partly by the way the light shone gold through his fins. They rippled and shimmered like very fine spun silk.

Everything seemed to slow down once more, and I was caught there, with my mouth hanging open. When the Fin King spoke his voice was slow and echoing as if he was speaking into a huge empty jar.

'Where is she?' he boomed.

There was a terrible silence. I knew, deep down, that he meant Anemone. But I shut the thought out, slammed a door on it inside my brain.

'Wh . . . who . . . ?' I stuttered feebly.

He glared at me. It felt as if the two of us were the only beings alive in the whole universe, and he was about to eat me, swallow me down into his watery stomach with all the smelly old half-digested fish.

'Only the daughter of the Sea Queen has tears like that!' he roared. He was angry I realised, but I didn't know why. Angry and probably dangerous. Desperately I glanced at Yan Eye out of the corner of my eye.

But Yan Eye said nothing and stared intently into space.

I tried to think of something to say. I was really scared the Fin King would swoop down on me at any second.

'Who's the daughter of the Sea Queen?' I asked, trying to sound innocent. I knew already. It was stupid to ask, but I just couldn't think of anything else to say.

Oddly it was Yan Eye who came to the rescue, even though he only said one word.

'Anemone,' he said. Quite clearly and distinctly. The word rang out in his soft lilting voice for all to hear. But at least it drew the Fin King's attention away from me.

He whirled round to face Yan Eye. 'How do you know her name?' he roared angrily. He stared at Yan Eye and for a moment he paused and looked really puzzled, as if he half recognised him.

'Who *are* you, Human? Speak!' he thundered. 'What brings you to Hildaland?'

But Yan Eye said nothing. He just stared back at the Fin King. He stared so hard that I thought his one eye must surely bore right through to the back of the Fin King's head.

Then Yan Eye nodded, in a quiet, dignified way, almost as if he were the king. 'Greetings, *brother*,' he said. I was amazed – was he mad? Surely they couldn't be *brothers*? Yan Eye must be about a hundred years older than the Fin King . . .

The Fin King seemed to hesitate for a moment, still staring at Yan Eye, and then his face darkened, almost as if a shutter had come down over it. He whirled round again, turning his back on Yan Eye. 'You are not my brother! No insolent mortal could ever be a brother of mine!' he roared. 'Take him to the Cave of Slime!'

Instantly two large Finmen came up behind Yan Eye and seized him. He began to struggle, and I could see he was trying to get his hands up to wrench off his scarf. I realised he was trying to show the Fin King his gills to prove he was not a mortal!

'I *am* your brother! Let me prove to you who I am!' he yelled. But it was no good – the two Finmen pinned his arms to his sides. He still tried to struggle out of their grasp and he snarled through clenched teeth. 'You will pay for this, Haldor!'

But the Fin King just ignored Yan Eye's words and kept his back turned. The Finmen dragged Yan Eye away, still struggling and cursing until they vanished through the great wooden doors.

I felt all trembly then, left standing there in front of the Fin King. Yan Eye hadn't been much use, but he was better than nothing. Now I was all alone and I felt suddenly very small and conspicuous.

There was a long, damp silence. The Finmen seated around the room coughed and shuffled. Then the Fin King sat back down on his throne and gave me this ghastly creepy smile. He held his hand out and spoke in a horrid, greedy, whispery voice: 'Come here then, little girl – give me the pearl that you hold in your hand!'

Well, I wasn't having that, was I? No way! Not now, after the way he'd treated Yan Eye and me! King or no king, he wasn't nicking Anemone's tear off me! This was the burst of anger I needed – up until that moment I'd been rooted to the spot, terrified by the Fin King and all his creepy Finmen. Quick as a flash, before anyone could stop me, I dodged behind Purple Fins and straight out of the open throne room doors.

I ran like the wind, sliding and skittering all the way across the damp floor of the great hall. I could hear Green Fins and Purple Fins behind me, bursting out of the throne room and running after me.

It all happened so fast I didn't have time to look where I was going at all. I just ran blindly into the nearest doorway, like a mouse looking for a hole in the skirting board when a cat's after it, clinging on to my pearl for dear life.

A corridor opened up in front of me, but it wasn't the one we'd come in through. It was narrower and it had bends in it. I was glad of those, because they kept me out of sight. But the Finmen were gaining on me – I could hear the horrible flap, flap of their feet pounding along the corridor in pursuit.

There were doors all along on either side, but I didn't

dare stop to open one and go in to hide, because it would slow me down too much. So I just kept on running. The corridor began to slope downhill slightly and my feet slipped more than ever.

Then I got to a place where the corridor branched off in three different directions. I was getting totally out of breath by then, so I just dashed down one of them without stopping to think, hoping the Finmen would go a different way.

If I didn't stop soon for breath my lungs would burst. Thankfully I saw a dark opening in the wall to my right. It was small and low down. Too small for a grown-up Finman to get in.

I slithered in and crouched in the opening out of sight. It was completely dark behind me and my imagination whispered to me that there could have been all sorts of monsters. But I didn't get out again, because I could hear the Finmen talking at the place where the corridor branched.

They sounded out of breath too – and they were angry, I could tell by their raised voices. I hunched further into my hole. Please let them go a different way, I breathed silently.

They must have decided to split up. I heard one set of webbed feet pounding away from me. Thank goodness. But then, horror of horrors, another set was coming down my corridor. I was sure to get caught if I came out.

I didn't want to get caught – they might send me to the Cave of Slime with Yan Eye! I didn't like the sound of that at all. It would be cold and damp, and they'd give me raw fish to eat for supper. If they gave me anything.

So I turned round and began to crawl, as fast and as silently as I possibly could, into the velvety blackness. My eyes strained wide open, but I couldn't see a thing. I just had to feel my way on my hands and knees.

I felt shivery. The tunnel I found myself crawling along grew colder and slimier all the time and I could feel water soaking into the knees of my jeans. It felt as if invisible things were standing there in the dark right in front of me, looking at me. I might bump into one at any moment.

Where on earth was this tunnel going? It seemed to be getting narrower too. Or was it my imagination? I was sure the ceiling was gradually getting lower. I might get *stuck* in there for ever and turn into a horrible skeleton.

Maybe I should turn round and go back? For a moment I panicked totally, and tried to turn around in the dark. But the tunnel was too narrow and I couldn't even get my head round. In any case – what was the use? The Finmen were back there!

I kept on crawling, my breath coming in ragged sobs. Then I had a good idea. I pretended I was Anne Bonny, searching a watery cave for hidden treasure. For a minute or two I felt a bit less scared and managed to crawl on.

But it didn't work for long. Playing at being Anne Bonny was OK normally – but this was *really* happening. I was myself – all alone, lost in a horrible dark tunnel. And it was about to get even worse. A *whole* lot worse . . .

. . . I heard this watery, slapping, snuffling noise behind

me. At first I tried to pretend I hadn't heard it. But it was getting louder. *Something* was coming along the tunnel. And it was catching me up fast.

Chapter Fifteen

The Monster

I've never crawled so fast in all my life! The sound of that thing coming up behind me made me gallop along so fast my knees quickly got sore banging down on the tunnel floor and once or twice my arms shot out from under me.

The slapping, slithering sound was getting nearer all the time. I shuddered to think what the heck the thing was that was making it. It couldn't be a Finman – they were too big to get into the tunnel.

Up ahead it was still pitch black and I was really scared of crawling slap bang into a stone wall. But the fear of the thing behind me was worse.

My arms and legs began to get really wobbly. So I was very glad when I realised that there seemed to be a faint glow of light ahead. I wobbled on, longing to stop, and the light grew brighter. I was actually coming to the end of the dark tunnel. Only a little bit further . . . I put on a last desperate burst of speed, came round a slight bend in the tunnel and – oh no . . . !

The tunnel ended in a narrow little gap! Was I going to be able to get through? Hastily I shoved my head in, plus one outstretched arm and then began frantically to wriggle the rest of my body through.

It was a really tight squeeze around my chest and for a moment I felt that ghastly panic about getting stuck again. I scrabbled and kicked my legs and wriggled some more, all the time knowing that the *whatever it was* must be right behind me and might grab my legs at any moment, and then at *last* I fell through . . .

. . . and shot out suddenly into brilliant sunshine. I fell briefly, arms and legs flailing in the air, until I landed with a soft whump in a huge pile of . . . gruegh!

It was seaweed partly. But it was also fish bones. Neat, picked clean skeletons, like you see in cartoons when the cat's been eating a fish. Fish heads too, and the odd tail fin.

It was totally disgusting, but I was so exhausted that I sank back into it gratefully, and lay there looking up at the blue sky while my lungs heaved in air and my arms and legs slowly began to calm down.

For a moment I totally forgot about the floppy, swishy thing that had been following me – I was so relieved to be out of the Finmen's palace. Only for a moment though.

Next thing I knew, something was sort of weaving and pressing around my legs. My knees were bent up and what-ever it was was slithering through the arch of my legs. It felt cool and wet. It was making a weird noise too.

It was kind of purring. Well not exactly . . . can you imagine what a cat would sound like if it was purring *underwater*? Well it sounded like that. Honestly.

Hardly daring to move I bent my neck up slowly to look at whatever it was that was making the sound. When I saw it I nearly freaked out altogether. I was getting used to strange animals in Hildaland, but this one really took the biscuit.

It was a blue-green fish with cat's legs. Tabby ones. It had cat's ears too – and whiskers – but its tail was a fish tail and it had a big sticking-up fin on its back.

It was very friendly. I think it was hoping that I'd produce a fish for it. I began to stroke it, and it went all kittenish and rolled over on to its back so I could stroke its tummy.

'Sorry, Kitty,' I said, 'I didn't bring any fish.' I tickled it under its fishy chin. Well – the place where its chin would have been if it had had one.

So that was the monster that had been following me down the tunnel, I thought. It was a – a *catfish*! It was nothing like the catfish in Cal's fishtank though – that's only about five centimetres long and it's just a fish with whiskers. But there was no doubt at all that this *must* be a catfish – anyone could see that!

I began to laugh with relief because it was so silly and because the *whatever it was* wasn't really a monster at all. And I realised I had just left the palace through a catfish flap for goodness' sake!

I stood up then and began to brush all the seaweed and stuff off me. Horrid little fish bones and scales were clinging to my clothes. I must have stunk like the harbour on a bad day.

The catfish continued to purr and weave itself around my legs. Then all of a sudden it trotted off away from the palace. When it had gone a short distance it turned round and stared at me in a determined sort of way.

'*Miaow!*' It said, in a bubbling fish-cat, catfish voice. '*Miaow!*' It looked me straight in the eye. I was sure for some reason that it meant for me to follow it. Just at that moment, I heard a distant shout and, looking round, I saw three Finmen running towards us. They must be all over the place looking for me, I thought!

They were shaking their arms and they didn't look too pleased. The catfish saw them too. 'Miaow,' it went again, urgently this time.

'OK, Kitty, I'm coming!' I said. I followed it off the mound of stinky stuff and I saw it was heading for another dark tunnel entrance, very like the one we had just emerged from. *Not again*, I thought.

But I had no choice really. The Finmen were getting really close. Close enough for me to hear their nasty webbed feet squishing across the grass. The catfish vanished inside the tunnel and I bent down to follow.

To my utter horror I saw that the tunnel led straight down into a dark pool of water. I just saw the tip of the catfish's tail splash into it and swim away.

I didn't know what to do, and for a moment I stood there staring hopelessly at the pool of water. The Finmen were incredibly close now; so close I could hear the gasp of their breath and smell the stale fishy waft of it.

It was either the pool or being taken prisoner. I chose the pool. I took a huge deep breath in and out several times, the way Alex and I do when we practise staying underwater at the swimming pool.

And then I dived in. I began to swim along underwater and then before I knew it I was swimming like a fish. How I breathed underwater I don't know, but I did. The water seemed to flow in and out of my nose just like I was breathing air as normal. It was easy. But please don't try it yourself – it only works if you're on Hildaland, and you'd just get a choking lungful of water if you tried. I know, because I once tried it in the swimming pool at home and I came up spluttering – it was awful.

I swam fast, really fast, not like I normally do, underwater. I could see perfectly well too, because there seemed to be light coming into the tunnel from above.

The water was a beautiful turquoise-blue colour, and there was waterweed all around me, in soft lacy fans that waved in the currents I made as I swam. Up ahead I could see the catfish. Its furry tabby legs were tucked in flat and its fishy tail was moving its body effortlessly though the water.

Where we were going I didn't know. I just followed the catfish's tail.

Chapter Sixteen

Elementary Magic

We seemed to swim for ages along the tunnel. But I didn't mind. I was back in the odd half-dream, half-awake state that I was getting so used to in Hildaland.

It wasn't hard work either, even though we went a long way. In fact, I was beginning to enjoy being a . . . what was I . . . was I a *fish*?

This thought startled me so much that I woke up suddenly from my in-between state and saw that the tunnel was rising up, quite steeply now, towards a circle of bright light.

I could see things above the water. Ordinary everyday things like seaweed-covered rocks and blue sky with fluffy white clouds. It was really odd looking at them from below the surface, as if the ordinary world was another, unknown world, different from how it was normally.

My eye caught a flash of silver then and I saw something like a large fishy tail dangling into the water above me.

Silvery bubbles of air clung to the scales and streamed upwards as the tail moved.

Next thing I knew I burst out of the water, coughing and spluttering just as if I'd stayed too long under at the swimming pool. I hauled myself out on to the seaweedy rocks, gasping for breath. And there, sitting beside me dangling her tail into the water, was Anemone!

She had the catfish on her knee and was stroking it and laughing. It rolled over and dabbed at her with its claws, just the way an ordinary cat would.

Anemone gasped when she saw me shoot out of the water. 'Rosie! You gave me a fright jumping out like that! Are you OK?'

'I think so – I got away from the Finmen and then I swam . . .' My voice trailed off. I realised I'd just shot up out of a *rock pool*. 'How could I *do* that . . . ?' I began, but Anemone cut me off short.

'It's Hildaland. It's different here. It's magic. You can swim underwater and *I* can move in the air . . .' She stood up. If a mermaid *can* stand up. What I mean is she sort of reared up on her tail. Then she lifted it gracefully up into the air and proceeded to fly, just like I'd seen some of the Finchildren do.

Honestly – that's how it looked. I guess she was kind of swimming really. But it looked like flying, because she was doing it in the air. If it was air, I thought, suddenly remembering the fields full of sea anemones and the strange grazing mer-cows and the wafting Finman gills.

It was very confusing. Anemone must have noticed me looking baffled. 'You look like a brain-dead sea-cucumber,' she said rudely. 'What's the matter?'

'It's this place – it makes me feel odd. I don't know when I'm on land and when I'm underwater and . . .'

Anemone interrupted with a scornful *pshaw* kind of noise and broke into peals of laughter. 'You humans are so *thick*! The air is water and the water's air and both are both at once. It's *perfectly simple* – don't you *see*?'

But I didn't. I was just getting even more muddled. No wonder being in Hildaland had made me feel so woozy when I first arrived! I couldn't grasp it at all. 'Oh *look*,' said Anemone impatiently. 'Can't you see this is *water* to me and *air* to you?' She swam, or flew, three times right around me until I felt totally dizzy. I nearly fell back into the rock pool. Had I really just swum up out of that? And if so – how come all my clothes were perfectly dry? Surely they should be soaking wet? I *still* didn't see. I didn't see *at all* and it was giving me a headache.

Anemone saw my puzzled face and laughed. It was a beautiful rippling sound like running water. 'Don't worry, Rosie – you'll get used to it!' She did a perfect somersault then, turning right over in mid-air just to show off.

I gave up trying to understand. I looked around and realised then that I was back on the beach, close to where we had landed. In fact there was Yan Eye's boat, drawn up on the shingle.

'Were you hiding in the bottom of the boat when the

Finmen came?' I asked, suddenly realising what must have happened.

'Yes. Under that smelly old blanket. I made myself quite see-through too.' As she spoke, Anemone sort of shimmered all round her edges and then faded slowly until I could see the beach pebbles through her – like I had before when Yan Eye and I had missed spotting her.

It made me feel scared for some reason. It was like everything in this strange world – so unpredictable and odd. 'Stop it!' I yelled. 'I hate it when you do that!'

Anemone came visible again suddenly. She laughed some more, but this time I could tell she was making fun of me. 'Nah nah nee naah nah – can't catch me!' she mocked, starting to fade again.

But I was too quick for her this time. I dived on her and grabbed her by the hair while I could still see where she was. She *felt* solid enough!

'Ow!' she yelled. 'Let go! You're hurting me!'

I was *really* narked with her. 'Don't mess me around then!' I yelled back fiercely. 'Don't mess with Anne Bonny!'

She came really solid then and kind of stared at me pityingly. 'Don't be such a prat! You're not Anne Bonny – I *knew* Anne Bonny!'

I just stared back at her. How could she have known Anne Bonny? But then I remembered how she'd said she was six hundred and something . . . I felt a real idiot then. I let go of her hair.

Anemone winced and rubbed her head. 'Look – I'm

sorry, OK? But I had to go see-through. I didn't want the Finmen to get me. I don't want to be a sad Finwife!'

'So how come you could go see-through again all of a sudden? Why on earth didn't you do that when Yan Eye came along and found you on the beach?'

She looked a bit embarrassed for a moment. 'Shut up!' she hissed, showing her sharp fang-like teeth.

But I wasn't letting her get away with it. 'Well, *why* then?'

'I tried if you *must* know,' she snapped. 'I'm only up to grade three in Vanishing. I can't always manage it fast enough. Anyway,' she added in a superior voice, 'don't forget I was drying out. It takes *energy*, you know!'

'Why did you not go invisible and swim home in the first place then?' I asked her crossly. 'You'd have saved us both getting into all this trouble!'

She sneered at me again. I'd begun to notice that she did this whenever she was feeling got at. 'What *do* they teach you in human schools? Don't they even teach you *elementary* magic? Vanishing? Manifesting?'

'No. They don't. It's not *my* fault.'

All this time the catfish was weaving around Anemone's tail making its fat furry bubbling noise. She sat down again and pulled it back on to her knee, tickling its furry tummy with her pale webbed fingers. 'Silly old Rosie,' she murmured. '*We* know don't we, Cocklepuss?'

Anemone was obviously getting cross, so I tried to back off a bit. 'Is that his name – Cocklepuss?' I said, bending down to stroke his ears.

'Cocklepuss, Cocklepuss, furry little Cocklepuss,' she chanted soppily, pressing her face into the furry bit of him. Then she looked up at me. 'I can't go invisible for very long – it uses up too much strength and I would need that for swimming. It's a long way without a sea horse, you stupid mortal,' she added with a pout.

That really bugged me – just when I was trying to be *nice* to her! 'Don't talk to me like I'm thick!' I snapped angrily. 'You're not so clever yourself – why didn't you just swim off home from the boat – get away while you had the chance and the Finmen were busy with me and Yan Eye?'

Anemone fiddled with her hair and pursed up her mouth into a tight little rosebud. 'I couldn't just *leave* you here – even if you *are* a stupid human. There is such a thing as honour among merfolk you know. You saved me and so I have to hang around and try to save you!'

'Huh,' I said crossly. 'Haven't *done* much then have you – just sat around preening yourself?'

'Who do you think sent Cocklepuss to guide you out of danger?' replied Anemone, quite unconcerned, shaking her hair out in a long shimmering wave.

I glared at her. She wasn't trying to help me to be *kind* – it was just some weird sense of duty thing. And anyway, I was still angry with her because she'd made me look like a loser. 'How do you do it then?' I demanded. 'Go see-through, I mean?'

Anemone grinned and, dumping Cocklepuss down on the shingle, she stood up on her tail again. She stretched out her arms and began to rotate slowly. 'Practice,' she said rather smugly. 'Practice and skill.' She reminded me of Melissa showing off her tap-dancing – when she goes all superior and shows off all the steps she knows. Like you *want* to know that stupid stuff. She wishes.

'You just let yourself go all frilly round the edges,' she added, 'and then you imagine yourself slowly fading away . . .'

Just then there came a horrible sound. One that froze us both to the spot. It was the unmistakeable squishy, wet sound of Finmen running towards us over shingle. How on earth could we have messed about for so long and forgotten that we were in danger? Then I heard the Finmen shouting to one another. They'd obviously spotted us and it was far too late to hide.

Cocklepuss fluffed up his furry bits and the fin on his back stood up all sharp and angry-looking. Then he dashed off up the beach and disappeared somewhere behind a bank of shingle and seaweed.

'Quick,' yelled Anemone, 'into the boat!' She nearly yanked my arm off, dragging me towards the sea where the *Hildaland* still lay at the edge of the shingle.

I scrambled into the boat as fast as I could and Anemone shoved it off the shingle so it was floating in the shallows. Suddenly Purple Fins and Green Fins were right there, at the top of the beach, not a hundred metres away.

They looked very out of breath and cross, and they were carrying long spears with barbed spikes on the end. I didn't like the look of *those* at all! Purple Fins reached under his glittering tunic and pulled something out.

It was a long, thin gold horn. He lifted it to his lips and blew. The sound was unearthly – high, long and thin like the horn that made it.

For a moment I was entranced by the beautiful sound of the horn. But then I realised that it was a signal. More Finmen guards in their glittering green and gold uniforms were coming, running along the shore towards us on their flapping feet.

It wasn't until I heard a strange bubbling neighing sound in the distance that I realised just how much danger we were in. It was soon followed by a rumbling of carriage wheels and then, bursting suddenly into view, there came a great golden chariot, pulled by two giant mer-horses.

The horses were blue-green and they had scales instead of hair. Their manes were made of flowing seaweed and instead of rear legs they had muscular fishes' tails that thrashed to and fro.

The hooves on their front legs thundered just like any horse, and their great tails made a terrifying noise like thick whips beating the air. They rushed straight down the beach and then shuddered to a halt near the edge of the sea, steaming and dripping.

I didn't like their red eyes. They kept rolling them back, showing the whites like they were driven and scared. Their mouths were fish mouths but they panted gusts of horsey breath.

Then I saw who was seated in the chariot, holding a long

whip. It was the Fin King. He looked as mad as a demon, with his eyes blazing and his wild gold hair streaming in the wind. And he was staring at Anemone like he was about to devour her.

Chapter Seventeen

Out of the Frying Pan, Into the Fire

I was dead scared. Standing there in his golden chariot at the edge of the sea, the Fin King seemed to tower above us like a vengeful giant. I was glad his chariot had wheels, so it couldn't go on the sea!

'Quick,' shouted Anemone, thrusting an oar at me, 'row for your life!' For a moment I couldn't move a muscle, but I began to feel the *Hildaland* move and glancing down I saw Anemone sitting with the other oar, frantically splashing it in and out of the water.

There was no time to lose. I bumped down on the seat beside her and, thrusting my own oar into the sea, we began to row frantically together. The oar was big and heavy and the first few strokes I took I didn't dip it far enough into the water and it just skittered uselessly along the surface.

I angled my oar more steeply into the sea then and hauled on it for all I was worth. It bit through the water and

I felt the boat begin to move. But slowly, oh so slowly, like we were rowing through treacle. And all the while more Finmen were rushing down the shore towards us, waving their dangerous-looking spears and shouting.

I saw the nearest ones fling down their spears, throw off their cloaks at the edge of the sea and begin to wade into the water. At least they weren't going to kill us with the spears, I thought with relief – but I suspected that they'd be swift as dolphins once they got fully into the water.

I could see their beautiful fins shimmering and sparkling under their arms. They were fanning them out slowly, ready to slice through the waves. We were done for. We'd soon be dragged off to the Cave of Slime!

'Capture them!' roared the Fin King. And he cracked his long whip with a sound like lightning tearing through the clouds in a great storm. His golden hair boiled around his head and his cloak streamed out behind him in the wind, revealing his glittering fins.

Two of the Finmen dived into the water, right under a breaking wave. I could see them coming at us underwater, their bodies as streamlined as seals and moving just as fast.

Then suddenly they surfaced right beside us and seemed to just hang there in the water, staring out to sea. They reminded me even more of seals then, the way they poked their heads out to look around.

There were several more Finmen just in the act of throwing off their cloaks at the edge of the sea, ready to dive in. They stood stock-still suddenly too, still holding their cloaks like they'd been frozen in time. Everyone seemed to be looking out to sea at something behind our tiny boat. Even the Fin King's expression had changed to one of amazement.

Just at that moment there came a weird tearing, sucking sound and suddenly the shore began to move away from us. I couldn't make out what was going on at all. One moment we were centimetres away from the clutches of the nearest Finman and then the shore just took off, like an express train, and hurtled away from us at breakneck speed.

It took me a few moments to realise that of course it was *us* moving and not the shore. We were streaming backwards across the waves at an astounding speed, leaving a huge white frothy wake behind us. The force of the sudden movement jerked us both off balance and we tumbled off our seat into the bottom of the boat in a heap of legs and fishy tail.

Both the oars were wrenched from our hands and fell overboard into the water. But it didn't make any difference, because there was no way either of us would have been strong enough to row against the force that had seized us.

'What's going on?' I blurted as soon as I could draw breath and began to pick myself up off the bottom of the boat. Was Anemone working some powerful escaping spell she'd learned at mermaid school?

But no – she was as astonished as I was.

'I've no idea. Look at that lot.' She giggled nervously, clinging on to the edge of the boat for dear life as she hauled herself up to look at what was happening. She was pointing to the row of gaping Finmen standing on the shore.

I had to laugh too, in a hysterical kind of way – they all looked so silly, standing there like a lot of idiots as we hurtled madly away across the water. Huge waves were crashing into the boat and soaking us, but I didn't care. 'Ha ha!' I yelled victoriously, wiping salty water out of my eyes with my sleeve. 'Can't catch us!'

I turned to grin at Anemone and saw her face was drained of all colour – not even a shred of pale green was left. She was looking *behind* us now. She didn't speak – she just pointed upwards with a trembling hand. Her eyes were like two great round staring marbles. I looked.

There, fastened firmly to the bow of the boat, outlined against the sky, was a *huge* tentacle. It had gleaming wet suckers all along it, as big as dinner plates. I gulped. I wasn't too keen to see what was joined to that tentacle.

'What . . .?' I mouthed. But Anemone put her finger to her lips to indicate that I should be silent. She was pulling herself along, inching towards the edge of the boat to take a look. It was really hard to move at all because of all the bumping up and down and the waves crashing in on us.

Trembling from head to foot I dragged myself up too, with arms that felt like they were made of useless cotton wool. And what I saw turned all my insides to jelly.

The island had vanished completely. There was just a smudge of mist on the horizon to show where it had been, and everywhere else was a huge expanse of ocean with frothy white waves. And stretched out for what seemed like half a mile in front of us was the great dark bulk of the body of something that was swimming very fast and dragging us along behind it with an enormous tentacle the colour of pond-slime.

I wasn't sure for a moment which was worse. Finmen or this – what *was* it? But before I had time to think about it too clearly the thing suddenly stopped swimming and let go of the boat with a schluping, schlurping noise like Alex rudely drinking the last little bottom bit of a can of Coke with a straw. Only ten million times bigger of course.

The thing reared itself up in the water then and glared at us, taller than a house. It had a horrid parroty kind of beak and two enormous eyes like cosmic black holes. The beak gushed sea water in a huge pouring stream and seemed poised, opening slowly, ready to tear us into minced meat.

I didn't have time to count its tentacles, but there seemed to be hundreds of them. They were all writhing and boiling about like a huge nest of demonic snakes.

And then the great curved beak was lurching towards us. It caught the sun for an instant and gleamed, like polished steel. To my amazement we began to move once more. I thought for a moment the sea monster was dragging us along again, but this time it was different. Slowly at first, though gathering speed every moment, we moved, not in a straight line this time, but in a slow spiral.

It was just like a gigantic, humungous bath plug opening up in the sea. And we were whirling down into it, like a tiny little helpless fleck of froth stuck to the towering glassy wall of the ocean.

Anemone opened her mouth and began to scream. A long, thin, hopeless, endless scream, like a ship's siren far out to sea. And then we were sucked faster and faster, down, down, down into the depths of the sea.

Chapter Eighteen

Ginny Greenteeth

It was like being on one of those rides at the fair that goes round so fast you feel sick and everything turns into a dizzy blur of lights and music. But it was massively vaster and more powerful.

I clung to the side of the boat – it seemed to be kind of tilting over, threatening to tip us out into the bottomless well of water. And there was this nightmarish rushing, sucking noise like being swallowed down an enormous throat.

I made the mistake of looking upwards then and I saw this appalling funnel of green water towering above us, and above that the sky, all blue with fluffy little clouds as if everything was perfectly normal. I was so scared then that I think I finally blacked out.

Next thing I knew, all the whirling round and round had stopped. I just lay there for what seemed like ages and then at last I cautiously opened my eyes. I was lying on a bed, of sorts, although it seemed rather damp and prickly. My head was propped on something soft.

I turned my head slightly to see what my pillow was made of. It was yellow and fluffy and it looked like a massive bath sponge. And the damp prickly stuff I was lying on was pink and white seaweed like the kind you find in rock pools.

I looked around and saw I was in a small round room, with a curved window of glass of the most beautiful pale blue above my bed. Just across the room was another bed the same size as the one I lay on. It was next to a large curved patio door that stood open, letting in what I thought at first was a light breeze that gently wafted the lacy cream curtains that framed the window.

Anemone was on this other bed, and someone was bending over her, mopping her forehead with a big piece of flat brown seaweed.

The someone was tall, very thin and clearly female. I couldn't see her face. She had long, dark green, matted hair, and the mottled hand that held the brown seaweed had long bony fingers and pointed nails. Not only that, but they were webbed, like a frog's hands.

Just then Anemone moaned and her eyes flickered open. I saw them widen then and a look of horror came over her as she saw who was there.

'Ginny Greenteeth!' she yelled, sitting up abruptly and balling herself up tight into a curl against the wall. 'Get off me, you evil hag!'

I must have let out a little yelp of fear too at this name, for the figure turned then and stared straight at me. You know what a frog's eyes are like? Golden and bulging? Well, they're OK on a frog – but not on a person. In fact, on a person they are *horrid*.

Ginny Greenteeth stared at me with her unblinking, glistening eyes. I felt like a fly must feel the moment before the frog's tongue flicks out and gulps it down. I stared back, unable to move a muscle.

And as I stared at her to my horror she *did* flick her tongue out. It was long and green and pointed. But all she did was to lick her right eye and then snap her tongue back in again. The licked eye glistened.

I knew all about Ginny Greenteeth. Everyone did. Dad always made out he knew this bloke who had actually seen her when he went fishing on South Beach late one summer night. She was sitting on Tom Hurd rock in the moonlight, singing a sad song about drowned sailors and combing her long green hair. A likely story!

All the kids knew about her too, and we played that if you accidentally trod on a crack between paving slabs near the harbour she would reach out a skinny arm from the nearest drain and drag you down. Then she would suck all the marrow from your bones and every drop of blood from your body.

Dad swore that this was true – it had happened to him on his way home from the pub one Friday night. He'd got away, but he was good for nothing all the next day. He kept moaning and telling us not to open the curtains.

When I was little I thought this was because he was scared Ginny Greenteeth would peer in at him and see him lying there on the sofa. But of course, since I got older, I'd realised he just had a hangover. I understood that Ginny Greenteeth was just made up to stop kids going near the harbour at night.

So what the heck was I seeing now? Surely she couldn't be *real*? Real or not, I didn't fancy Ginny Greenteeth touching *me*. If she *was* real, maybe the stories about her sucking all your blood out and that were real too!

I leaped up and backed into a corner. 'Get off her!' I yelled. 'Leave her alone!'

To my surprise Ginny Greenteeth didn't flick out her tongue again and swallow me. She just stared at me with her froggy eyes and began to laugh! It sounded like quite a kind sort of laugh, but her green teeth showed and they looked long and sharp.

When she stopped laughing she stood there, hands on hips, and said, 'Why bless you, child. I won't harm you or your friend! Your tea's ready. Come into the garden!'

That was the last thing I'd expected her to say and I was so gobsmacked that I just stood there not knowing what to do. Meanwhile though, Anemone slid off her bed behind Ginny Greenteeth and made a bolt for the open patio door.

Ginny Greenteeth must have heard her, for she turned round to see where Anemone had gone. She laughed again then, and shook her head and clicked her tongue just like my gran would do. 'Come on,' she said, 'let's join her.'

Suddenly I didn't feel so scared of Ginny any more because I had been reminded of Gran. And the idea of tea being ready was suddenly a very good one. So I came out of my corner and followed her out of the door.

I was expecting to find myself in some horrible dank kind of place where a frog would live – with walls of green mildew and a floor of slippery rock. I wasn't prepared for a single moment for what I saw.

We were in the most beautiful garden I had ever seen. But instead of privet or lavender or hydrangeas, the shrubs and bushes seemed to be made of coral and seaweed in every imaginable colour. I could see soft pinks, deep reds, every shade of green, yellow and creamy, ivory white. There were compact coral bushes all covered in swirling patterns and tall, feathery corals like fans that waved gently as if stirred by an invisible current. And in and out of all the plants swam gorgeous *fishes* in bright blue, harlequin stripes of orange and white, and sizzling lemon.

The garden was circular and across at the far side I could see an archway, very like the rose arches you see in normal gardens – but this one was made of coral and covered in red and pink sea anemones. It seemed to lead through into another garden, but I couldn't really see what was in there.

We must be underwater, on the seabed, I thought. We got sucked down the whirlpool under the sea! So how come I can breathe? But I was getting used to this sort of thing since I'd been taken to Hildaland. It didn't seem quite so odd any more. Maybe it was all part of Ginny's magic.

In any case, I soon forgot about the weirdness of it all when I noticed a round table in the centre of the garden. It was piled up with food and set with plates made of huge oyster shells and pale cups that looked like mother-of-pearl, ready for drinks. I hadn't eaten since lunch time and suddenly I realised how hungry I was.

Chapter Nineteen

Tea With a Sea Witch

I bet you've never been invited to tea in a garden at the bottom of the sea! It was a mega feast and Anemone and I forgot to be afraid. We couldn't wait to get stuck into it all!

There were crab-shaped bowls, piled high with succulent tiger prawns and a huge bowl shaped like a fish, filled with a multicoloured salad of seaweed that to my surprise tasted absolutely delicious.

There were biscuits like seashells, and bowls of nibbles and dips and things that looked like curly crisps, only they were bright blue. There were things that looked like strawberries and apricots and slices of mango dipped in sugar.

In the centre was a massive cake shaped like a whale, with a huge spun-sugar spout of water coming from its blowhole. And best of all, we were allowed to eat anything we liked, in any order – Ginny didn't care.

Something brushed up against my leg while I was tucking

into the tiger prawns and looking down I saw it was another catfish. A black one this time, with shaggy black legs. I slipped it a morsel of prawn and it gulped it down gratefully and then sat mewing for more.

Eventually I felt I was getting full to bursting and I had to leave the last prawn on my plate and give it to the catfish. Just at that moment I noticed small frilly things were arriving, coiling up the legs of the table and swarming on to the bowls of food.

In no time at all there were dozens of them all over the place. They were like slugs only bigger, with brightly coloured wavy edges in blue, red, green and purple.

'Eugh!' I said, pulling a face and putting down the piece of whale cake I was eating.

'Don't worry,' laughed Ginny, seeing my look of disgust. 'They're only sea slugs! They've come to tidy up!' And sure enough, as we watched, the slugs were busily cleaning every plate until they were all sparkling and clean.

'You see!' said Ginny. 'You can't always judge by appearances! I'm not always hideous to look at either by the way,' she said. And she flicked her tongue out again and polished her left eye.

'What *else* do you look like then?' asked Anemone, cautiously swallowing a mouthful of a pink sea-horse-shaped biscuit that she'd rescued from the sea slugs.

'Look more closely!' said Ginny, with an odd little smile. We both stopped eating and watched her carefully. And then, just for an instant, I saw her differently, as if she was a beautiful young woman.

Her hair was no longer dark green and tangled like sea-weed washed up on the shore. It was pale green, straight and flowing down her back like a rippling waterfall. Her skin shone pearly white like moonlight – even on her hands it was smooth and unwrinkled.

It only lasted a moment, and then she was back in her ugly, froggy form. I blinked and stared, but I couldn't make her change back again. 'How did you do that?' I gasped.

Ginny grinned, flicking out her long tongue. 'I have more than one true form.' She laughed ruefully. 'But nowa-days most people can only see me *this* way – if at all.' She added sadly, 'If you are afraid, or if your heart is full of greed or anger, then you will only ever be able to see the scary side of me.'

Meanwhile Anemone had been staring at Ginny with-out speaking. She looked really gobsmacked, like she'd seen a ghost or something. 'You're *Ginny Spindrift*!' she exclaimed suddenly. 'Sea witch of all the Islands! I never knew you and Ginny Greenteeth were the same person – I didn't recognise you!'

Ginny smiled a wide froggy smile. 'There's a lot folk don't know about me,' she said mysteriously.

'She was engaged to Haldor!' explained Anemone, turning to me.

'The Fin King?' I said, amazed, remembering that this was the name Yan Eye had called him by.

Ginny nodded and wrung her webbed hands. 'Yes, she's

right. I was engaged to be married to Haldor, the Fin King.'

'And I was going to marry his twin, Flodraval,' said Anemone sadly. I stared at her – so she *had* been going to marry a Finman! Could it have been Yan Eye? But no – he was ages older than the Fin King, even though he had called him 'brother'.

'Starfish were busy weaving our wedding gowns,' said Ginny, 'from white seafoam decorated with tiny clusters of pink pearls.'

Blargh! This was getting *girly*. Anemone had this rapt, soppy expression – I had to change the subject and quick before a full-blown wedding dress conversation started!

'You're a *witch*?' I interrupted hurriedly, turning back to Ginny. 'A sea witch?'

Ginny nodded again. 'It was me that used to rescue sailors and steer them away from the dangerous shoals of rocks in stormy weather. All the sailors loved me in the days when they could see my beauty.'

'So do you do sea magic and stuff?' I asked.

'Of course. Who else do you think sees to everything? Who makes sure the moon is getting on with pulling the tides properly and the lobsters are laying their eggs? Who counts all the shrimps and checks the seaweeds are holding on to the rocks and —'

'But – what happened then – why did you not marry the Fin King?' I butted in again. I found it hard to imagine that Ginny Greenteeth had ever been about to marry the magnificent Fin King. But I *had* to know what had happened.

Ginny looked sad then. Her wide mouth drooped and she blinked her eyes slowly, as if blinking away tears. 'We were out swimming together one day,' she said. 'Haldor was so handsome and I was very much in love. I loved to watch his lithe athletic body as he swam in and out of —'

This was in danger of getting slushy again. 'Yes, yes,' I interrupted, 'but what *happened*?'

'We came to a place where a pirate ship was moored near a rocky cove.'

'A *pirate* ship?' I said excitedly. '*Cool.*' This was beginning to sound more interesting.

'We could hear an argument going on, so we swam up underneath the ship to watch and listen. Two of them were yelling at one another. "*It's mine!*" shouted one of them, a great big man with a black, bristling beard. But the other pirate, a tall thin man with straggly red hair, tied in a pony tail, was having none of it. "*Get off me!*" we heard him shriek. The two of them fell on one another then, and we could see them wrestling on the deck.'

'Who won?' I asked interestedly.

'Neither of them. The tall skinny one was pinned to the deck by the bulk of the big fat one. But he managed to raise his arm and hurl something into the sea. "*You fool,*" shouted the fat one. "*We'll never find it again – the water's fathoms deep here! We'll never get rich now!*" We saw something flash sparkling gold as it twisted and turned and sank down through the water. Haldor dived down after it to see what it was. He was so swift and —'

'But what was it?' I couldn't wait to find out!

'The thing lodged at last in a rocky cleft. Haldor seized it and swam back up to show me. It was a thin gold band, just the right size to fit on someone's head.'

I got a shivery feeling all of a sudden. As if I was half remembering something. But I didn't have time to think what, because Ginny carried on with the story.

'Haldor laughed. "*A new crown for the coronation.*" He and Flodraval were to be crowned kings together the following month and Anemone and I were to be brides together.'

'But it never happened,' sobbed Anemone, and tears began to pour down her face.

'Why not?' I put my arm around Anemone to comfort her. Weddings might be naff, but I felt quite sorry for her – it obviously mattered a lot to her.

'Haldor went mad,' she choked. 'He started to go crazy for gold and treasure and then . . .' she sobbed so hard she could hardly speak. 'He decided he wanted to marry *me* instead of Ginny!'

Chapter Twenty

Bordin's Band

'It was the gold band,' explained Ginny. 'It was bad magic. As soon as I set eyes on it, I knew it was a bringer of evil. But it was too late. Haldor plonked it straight on to his head and pretended it was a crown.

'As soon as it was on his head it shrank to fit so tightly that he couldn't get it off again. It sent tendrils of some ancient sorcery into his brain and he began to think of nothing except power and wealth and treasure.'

'He forgot all about poor Ginny, because she was not wealthy,' said Anemone. 'He fell right out of love with her and he got jealous of Flodraval because he was engaged to me.'

I gave her a blank look. This didn't quite make sense.

'I am the daughter of the Sea Queen, don't you know,' said Anemone in a very superior voice, staring at me with her great onyx eyes. 'Heir to the Throne of all the Oceans, including the lands of the Finmen. My wealth is unimaginable.'

I gaped at her. But I didn't have a chance to say anything.

'It was all Haldor could think of once that gold band was locked on to his head,' said Ginny with a damp, froggy croak. 'He wanted the power that such a marriage would bring him.'

'He turned into a kind of pirate – he would go sailing every day with bands of Finmen and take ships captive and ransack them – just for the riches they carried,' said Anemone. Huge tears began to roll down her cheeks. Now they were *both* in tears. What was I going to do? We'd all get drowned in tears at this rate!

'That's awful!' I cried. 'What happened then?'

'Haldor seized power,' said Anemone. 'He locked Flodraval up in the Cave of Slime and ruled Hildaland alone, even though he and Flodraval should both have been kings together. He demanded tribute from all quarters of the Fin Kingdom until his people grew to fear and hate him.

'He demanded my hand in marriage too, but I was afraid of him and I hated him for betraying Flodraval, so I refused him.'

'That was when he went totally insane,' said Ginny sadly. 'He was so full of rage and greed that he secretly used the evil gold band to put a terrible curse on his people. Nobody knew it was him that laid the curse except me – I watched him do it through my magic eye.'

'The curse of the Finwives you mean?'

'Yes. He decided that if he couldn't have a beautiful, happy wife then nobody else should either. Since then, all the Finwives have slowly grown depressed and miserable and no girl children have ever been born to the Finfolk . . .'

Anemone sank her head in her hands as Ginny spoke and began to cry again, even more floods than before! Hopeless great wracking sobs shook through her whole body.

'In the end, Haldor was so angry and jealous that he could not have Anemone's riches that he challenged Flodraval to a duel,' said Ginny. 'He pierced Flodraval's eye with a silver spear and he cursed him with the evil power of the gold band and banished him from Hildaland for ever!'

Something here was starting to make sense to me in a hazy kind of way – Flodraval had lost his eye in a duel and been banished from Hildaland . . . so maybe . . . 'But . . . why . . . why did you not *find* Flodraval and marry him any-way?' I asked Anemone. 'Surely he still loved you?'

Anemone looked up with tears streaming down her face. 'Because he vanished. Nobody has ever seen him since the day Haldor banished him from Hildaland.'

It was then, looking at the tears running down Anemone's face that everything just fell into place in my mind – *click!*

'Actually,' I said slowly – I still wasn't quite sure, but it *must* be right . . . 'I think I know where he is.'

Yan Eye and the Fin King. It was so obvious all of a sudden. They were more than just brothers. They were *twins*. I realised that this seemed really silly – the Fin King was young and beautiful and Yan Eye was an Old Git. But even so, somehow I *knew* . . .

'He's back in Hildaland. He's Yan Eye,' I said.

There was a silence and Anemone gaped at me. She looked very fishy, with her mouth hanging open. Like a cod. *Personally* I didn't think she was all that beautiful. But then I'm not a merperson or a Finperson.

'Yan Eye?' gasped Anemone. 'That *horrid old man*! That . . .' she gulped with distaste. 'That . . . *human*! It's not possible – how could you *think* such a thing? Just because he's got an eye missing too?'

But I *knew* it was true. Poor Anemone. I didn't know what to say. But I didn't have to say anything, because Ginny said it for me.

'Rosie's right.' Ginny nodded, thoughtfully. 'Living amongst mortal men for many years, Flodraval would grow to look like a human – and age as a mortal would.'

'He's still got his gills though!' I shouted excitedly. 'I've *seen* them!'

Anemone looked cross then. 'When? *When* did you see them?'

'In the boat . . .' I felt a bit scared the way she was staring at me.

'Why did you not *tell* me?'

'I didn't know who he was! I didn't even realise he was a

131

Finman until we were captured! I thought he was some kind of weird *fish thing*!'

Anemone glared at me. 'But why did *he* not tell me who he was?'

I didn't know the answer to this of course. 'Maybe he thought you would never believe him!' I suggested.

Anemone began to sob uncontrollably then. It was a horrible wailing sound that made me feel all lost and lonely and cold for a moment – until I realised how *soppy* she was being. Really *wet*. She would never get into the Harbour Gang and neither would I if I didn't think of something brave and sensible to do.

Suddenly I remembered the huge pile of treasure beside the Fin King's throne – the shining silver goblets, the ropes of gleaming pearls . . . what was it he had said?

I racked my brains. Then it came back to me. '*None of it's worth a herring to me any more*,' I muttered. Ginny and Anemone stared at me with their alien eyes.

'What did you say?' asked Ginny.

'*None of it's worth a herring to me any more.* That's what he said to me.'

'*Who?*' snapped Anemone, drying her eyes on a long strand of hair. 'You're talking utter gibberish.'

'The Fin King. Haldor,' I said slowly. 'He was talking about his treasure hoard. I think . . . I think he might be beginning to feel sorry for what he did!'

Anemone sniffed loudly. 'Huh!' she said scornfully. 'It's a bit late for that now!'

'There must be something we can do though,' I said. 'We can't just leave Yan Eye alone on Hildaland! He's locked up in the Cave of Slime!'

Anemone looked really horrified. Her eyes nearly popped out of her head. 'The Cave of Slime!' she yelled. 'Again! Why didn't you say so before?'

'Why – what do you mean?' I stuttered.

'He'll be left there to *rot*,' choked Anemone. 'What do you think the *slime* is made of?'

I gulped. Thoughts of the Dead House suddenly swam back into my head and I felt sick. Surely the Fin King wasn't *that* evil? 'But . . . but what can we *do*?'

Anemone was silent. She just stared at me helplessly. Neither of us could think of *anything*. It was Ginny who spoke next.

'There *is* something you can do,' she said, 'but it won't be easy.'

I leaped to my feet and pushed my chair back. 'I don't care *how* hard it is,' I yelled, 'I'm a pirate. I'm brave and fearless.'

Anemone gave me a pitying look. 'Oh *please*,' she said scornfully.

I felt a bit stupid then, but I glared back at her. I wasn't going to give up that easily. 'We'll go and rescue him! I'm not scared!' I was really of course – totally petrified – but I wasn't going to let a snobby mermaid get the better of me!

Anemone's expression seemed to change for a moment and she looked at me almost with a kind of respect. Maybe once you begin to believe in yourself other people begin to believe in you too.

But then her face fell and she looked sad again. 'But we can't go alone can we, Rosie – just the two of us? It would be really dangerous. We'd probably end up in the Cave of Slime too . . .'

'Ginny will help us!' I said excitedly. 'Won't you, Ginny?'

But Ginny shook her head. 'I can't go with you,' she said sadly. 'The golden band will warn Haldor of my approach to Hildaland.'

'*Warn* him?' I said. 'How?'

'The band will scream to warn its wearer if it feels my powerful magic coming close.'

'How do *you* know?' asked Anemone, sounding doubtful.

'After Haldor seized power, I wanted to find a way to release him from the grip of the evil gold band. I searched for many years, throughout all the islands, until I found out the story of who had made it.'

'Who was it?' I asked.

'A Finman called Bordin, hundreds of years ago. He was a great sorcerer. He grew very greedy and he forged the band as part of an evil spell to bring him great wealth.'

'A *spell*?' I gasped. 'You mean like —' but I never had time to ask more because Anemone interrupted me.

'What happened to him?' she asked eagerly.

'Well,' said Ginny slowly, 'the gold band *did* bring him great wealth, but after many years he realised his life was hollow and empty.'

'Like Haldor?' I said.

'Yes. He realised that he had enormous wealth but no friends and no one to love him. The gold band he had forged to bring him wealth turned out to be a terrible curse – and just like Haldor, he found that he couldn't take it off his head. He was trapped by his own greedy magic.'

'So what did he do?' I asked.

'In the end, after years of loneliness, he managed to get the band off his head.'

'How?' I asked. 'Why don't you tell Haldor how he did it?'

But Ginny just looked sadder than ever and swallowed loudly and froggily in her damp throat. 'I wish I knew. I've searched for years for the answer to that question. All I know is that he took it far from anywhere in his boat and hurled it into the sea, so that it could not harm anyone else.'

'Until those pirates found it!' I said. 'But why didn't Bordin just melt it down? After all, he made it in the first place!'

'The band has a primitive kind of life of its own,' said Ginny. 'It was part of the magic. If you try to throw it into fire it leaps out again and tries to burn you.'

She shuddered and looked away for a moment. 'As I said before, I can't come with you to rescue Yan Eye. But I *can* help you from afar. Follow me.'

She stood up from the table and walked towards the archway. Anemone just sat there for a moment, still gaping like a cod. Then she blinked and blew her nose suddenly on a seaweed handkerchief that Ginny had handed her.

'OK then, fine,' she said bravely. 'Come on, let's go. You'd only get caught, lost or in trouble without me. Probably all three.'

Chapter Twenty-one

Tangle and Dulse

The garden through the arch was circular like the first one, only smaller. The boundary was not of coral bushes this time, but a low rocky wall about a metre high. A beautiful path of crazy paving in polished deep green and blue tiles ran inside this wall so that you could walk right around.

But in the centre was a very strange thing. I couldn't make out what it was at all. It was a kind of hovering globe of light that seemed to shift and move with swirling rainbow colours, rather like an enormous soap bubble. As I watched, it drifted slightly to one side and then back again to the centre. It looked almost alive.

'It's a scrying bubble. My magic eye,' explained Ginny, seeing the baffled look on both our faces. 'You look into it and *see* things. That was how I saw Haldor lay his evil curse on the Finfolk and that was how I knew that you were in grave danger from the sea monster. It roams the sea in these parts, eating all it catches.'

I gasped. 'So it was *you* that made the whirlpool?'

Ginny nodded and laughed. 'It's an old trick I learned from my grandmother.'

'So this scrying bubble is a bit like a crystal ball?' I said, suddenly understanding what she meant. I'd seen Gypsy Gina using one at the fair that came to the harbour last year.

'Yes. Only it's not crystal. It's an air pool.'

'An *air* pool?' I couldn't quite get my head round this. I was still convinced that I was not underwater, but breathing air as normal – even though I could see fish darting around everywhere and the plants around me were all corals and seaweed.

'Yes. On land people scry into crystal or pools of water. We use pools of air.'

This made a warped kind of sense. 'Can we look in?' I asked, excited now by the idea of what I might be able to see.

'Yes. Come and sit down here and just let your mind drift as you look into the bubble.' Ginny pointed to a low bench made of the same stone as the wall. We all went and sat on it in a row, and for a moment I thought of the Old Git Gang sitting in their row of three on the harbour wall and felt a pang of wanting to be home and everything back to normal.

But it wasn't going to be that easy was it? Anemone was still far from home and Yan Eye was being held prisoner in the gruesome Cave of Slime. We had to find a way to rescue him.

At first I couldn't see anything but the swirling patterns

of rainbow colours. Slowly I let my eyes go unfocussed and then suddenly the bubble seemed to clear completely and I saw a picture in it, like watching a film.

It was Yan Eye. He was sitting all hunched and miserable on a slimy-looking floor of stone. Cold rocky walls surrounded him, with trails of green slime dripping down them.

'It's Yan Eye!' I yelled excitedly. 'In the Cave of Slime!' And as I shouted out the image vanished and I was back to looking at rainbow swirls again.

'Shh!' said Ginny. 'Just watch quietly . . .'

The swirls began to clear again and this time I seemed to be looking at a huge door. 'There's a door . . .' I began.

'I see it too! It's locked I think,' said Anemone, 'maybe it's the door to the Cave of Slime . . .'

We took Ginny's advice then and watched without speaking. The rainbow swirls faded away and I saw the door clearly. It was huge and black, with a grill at the top like a prison door and a massive, very forbidding-looking lock shaped like a big wavy oyster shell.

Just then there was a flicker of something over to the right of the picture. I only got a fleeting glimpse of it, but it looked like an enormous claw. Anemone gave a gasp of horror.

'Ugh! There's a *thing* . . . a huge . . . giant crab!'

'That's the guard,' said Ginny solemnly.

I whirled round and stared at her. She licked her eyes nervously and swallowed.

'The *guard*. But . . .'

'You have to get past it,' she added, licking her left eye again and staring at me in a very unnerving way.

'*Right*,' I said. 'Like . . . how?'

'Fish. You take fish,' said Ginny. I didn't quite get this, but before I had time to ask what she meant, she waved a mottled hand at me to be quiet and pointed back at the scrying bubble.

All I could see at first was water. White and bottle green, frothing and rushing like water coming over a weir. There were bubbles streaming through it, silver and shining, masses of them.

But as I watched, Ginny held her arms outspread above her head and she was chanting, strange words that I couldn't understand, with lots of clicks and whistles, a bit like dolphins speaking. Then I saw a huge animal slowly appearing right there in the air pool in front of me. Ginny was doing magic!

It was scaly and gold, gleaming like polished metal, but real and alive. I felt myself being lifted on to its back as if by some strange unseen force.

I saw there were tiny black dots, glinting under the skin, and a row of sharp golden spines rising in front of me along the arched neck of the beast. And then it turned its head and I saw a kind of horse's head, but with a long, thin, tube-shaped muzzle striped in black and white, and an alert black beady eye looking at me interestedly.

A sea horse! I realised with a sudden rush of excitement. I was on the back of a huge, golden sea horse! It wasn't at all like the horrible fierce mer-horses that thundered along pulling the chariot of the Fin King. It was a delicate, graceful creature, like the kind of sea horse I had seen in the Seaworld Aquarium, only much bigger.

I looked down and saw that there were reins in my hands then, and a beautiful red and gold saddle under me, that was specially curved and shaped to rest above the fin on the creature's back.

I twisted round to see the fin wafting gently in the water behind us, shifting in the flow of the current. It was like a beautiful gold and silver transparent fan. Then there was a snorting, bubbling neigh alongside me and, glancing across, I saw that Anemone was seated on a second sea horse. Hers was iridescent blue and she was seated sideways on a special side-saddle.

Both sea horses were rocking and twisting, plunging their necks up and down. I could feel the ripple of huge muscles all down the flanks of the one I was on, and I saw Anemone's horse uncurling and lashing its long tail. They were ready to be off.

Ginny was beside us, laughing and waving her thin arms. I could hardly make out what she was saying, with the rush and foam of the bubbles all around us and the impatient snorting of our sea horses.

'Hold him steady. His name is Tangle and he needs a firm hand,' said Ginny. Hold the reins like this, and grip hard with your knees . . .' And she showed me how to wrap the reins around my fingers and sit firmly in my seat.

'Here – you'll be needing this,' shouted Ginny then,

thrusting a bag made of pale green leathery stuff into my hand. There was something heavy in it, but I didn't have time to ask her what it was.

'Be off now! Swim with all speed, Tangle and Dulse!' yelled Ginny. And she slapped the flank of my sea horse so that it plunged forwards with a sudden lurch and we were off.

We rose up from the seabed and I could see Ginny's garden down below us. I could see her little round house and the air pool gleaming like a huge bubble.

I didn't have time to look down for long though – I had to put all my energy into staying on my sea horse! We were travelling very fast, and once or twice I nearly fell off and had to grab hold of the front of my saddle and make sure I didn't drop the reins or let go of the leather bag.

The odd moment I had a chance to glance alongside I could see Anemone, riding smoothly and serenely, seeming to glide along without the slightest difficulty. I felt a bit clumsy and stupid until I realised she had obviously had lots of practice.

'Don't worry, Rosie!' shouted Anemone. 'You'll soon get the hang of it! Just hold on tight!'

Every so often my sea horse snorted and huge streams of bubbles flowed past on either side of us. His beautiful golden neck rippled in front of me and when I had got my balance I patted him encouragingly. It was like patting a horse, but instead of being warm and furry his skin felt smooth and cold.

'Good boy, Tangle!' I yelled. I was starting to enjoy myself, as we sped along, coiling though masses of waving seaweed, plunging in and out of rocky underwater archways. 'Whooo! This is really *great*!' I shouted.

'Follow me!' yelled Anemone, swooping low underneath a mass of coral that made a pink and white bridge. I hardly had time to decide if Tangle and I would fit the small space, before I was rushing through too and coming up the other side.

We carried on, past a sinister stingray – black above and silver below, like a gigantic living carpet gliding along in the sea – then a shoal of green and blue striped fish that I recognised as mackerel. They changed direction and swerved all together like a single fish when they saw us coming.

Then suddenly we were swimming upwards. I could see the sky above us and before I knew it we burst through the surface of the sea and I could see a shore in front of us, just a few feet away, with small waves lapping in a white frothy frill at the edge.

And I realised, with a sickening lurch in my stomach, that we had reached the shore of Hildaland. The wonderful sea horse ride was over. It was time to go and rescue Yan Eye from the Cave of Slime.

Chapter Twenty-two

Into the Caves

Tangle and Dulse bent their necks forward in the shallow water and let us slide off their backs. Then they were gone, with a sudden whip and splash of their long coiling tails. All that was left of where they had been a moment ago was a mass of silvery bubbles on the surface of the sea.

We sat on the warm shore of multicoloured pebbles to get our breath back.

'What now?' I asked. 'Do you know how to get to the Cave of Slime?'

'No,' replied Anemone. 'All I know is that you get to it from a tunnel that runs underground from the palace. I've never been to it.'

'Maybe there's another way in?' I suggested hopefully. But before Anemone could reply there was a thin mewing, bubbly sound, and there was Cocklepuss!

'Hello, you're back again,' I said, leaning down to rub behind his furry cat's ears. 'Is he your catfish, Anemone? How come he always seems to turn up when we need him?'

'Of course he's not mine,' said Anemone in surprise. 'He doesn't *belong* to anyone. What an odd idea! He just lives in the palace that's all. He was very fond of Flodraval though. Before . . .' Her face crumpled and I was afraid for a moment that she might be going to start crying again. Not that I blamed her now that I knew what she'd been through.

'So that's why he's helping us then!' I said excitedly. 'He knows where Flodraval is, doesn't he?'

Cocklepuss rubbed himself against my legs and then sniffed interestedly at the green leather bag that I was still clinging on to. I'd forgotten about the bag until then.

I struggled with the chord that tied the neck of the bag and peered in. There was a fishy pong and I wrinkled up my nose.

'Ugh! It's full of bits of old fish! Yeuk!' I was about to fling the bag away in disgust when Anemone stopped me.

'Don't you see? It's for the crab guard. Crabs love smelly old fish and stuff.'

So did Cocklepuss. He sat in front of me purring loudly and hopefully. I picked a bit of fish out of the bag, trying not to touch it any more than I could help, and flung it down in front of him.

Cocklepuss chewed at the fish, gulped it down and then stood up, licking his whiskers. Then he began to walk away, turning round to look at us as he went.

'I think he wants us to follow him. Maybe he knows the way to the Cave of Slime?' I suggested. I got up, picked up the smelly bag of fish, and began to walk after Cocklepuss. He led us along the shore and then inland towards a crumbling cliff face.

You could see layers of rock in the cliff, all twisted and bent into strange shapes. Up above us there was a face made out of rock, like a miserable Finwife face with one staring eye wide open and the other all screwed up. I pointed to it and Anemone shuddered.

But Cocklepuss went right up to the cliff and then seemed to disappear. Following him we found a small crack in the rocky wall, like the narrow entrance to a cave. I didn't like the look of it much, but Cocklepuss seemed to know what he was doing, so I squeezed in through the crack and found myself in a rocky tunnel. The whole island seemed to be a maze of tunnels of one sort or another!

Anemone followed me and we hesitated nervously near the entrance, not wanting to move further in. It was very dark ahead of us – only a small patch of sunlight came in through the entrance, and after that there was this awful blackness and a steady sound of dripping water.

'What now?' whispered Anemone. 'I can hardly see a thing!'

But as we stood and wondered what to do it seemed to be getting lighter. At first it was just a dim glow, but slowly it grew, until the tunnel was lit by a pale green light. I gasped when I realised what was making the light.

'What *are* they?' I asked. For I could see hundreds and hundreds of little creatures, crawling everywhere over the surface of the rocky tunnel walls. They seemed to be all coming towards us, each adding his own tiny light to the others in order to light our way.

'They're glow lights,' said Anemone. 'They live in the caves – that's why they have bodies like glow-worms, that light up. They must be helping us too! Come on – there's Cocklepuss over there!'

He was waiting for us just ahead. He jumped up and began to run away along the tunnel, which sloped gently uphill. We began to follow.

The tunnel got narrower and the ceiling lowered gradually the further in we went. I shuddered, remembering the awful tunnel that I had crawled along to escape from the palace. I didn't fancy having to do *that* again.

The air seemed to be getting warmer and stuffier and it was hard to breathe. There was a nasty pong, like ancient pond water. Suddenly I remembered the giant crab guard. It could be anywhere in here . . . it could be right around the next corner waiting for us!

The tunnel twisted and turned and all the time I kept imagining that I could hear the scraping of the giant crab's shell scuttling in the dark. But it must have been the sound of my own feet scuffling along the floor.

Suddenly up ahead there seemed to be a dark mass. For a horrid moment I thought I could make out the outline of the giant crab lurking there, but as we got up to it we could see it was a huge jumbled rockfall blocking the tunnel. Cocklepuss squeezed through a small opening at the bottom of the pile and disappeared.

'Oh no,' said Anemone, hovering gloomily beside me. 'How are we going to get through *there*? We're far too *big*.' We could hear Cocklepuss mewing for us to follow, from the other side of the rockfall.

'Stupid animal!' snapped Anemone, rolling her huge dark eyes and flinging her long green hair behind her with an impatient flick. 'Come on, we'll have to find another way!' She whirled round in mid-air and began to go back the way we'd come. All I could do was follow her out of the cave.

We sat down on the shingle and wondered what to do next. The twisted face in the cliff sneered down, seeming to mock us for being so pathetic. I stuck my tongue out at it crossly.

At that moment I seemed to see something move in the shadow of its blank and staring eye. Then a faint *miaow* sounded from above.

'It's Cocklepuss!' I yelled, jumping up and pointing to the dark eye. 'There's a cave up there and he's calling us to go up!'

Anemone looked up to where I was pointing. We could see Cocklepuss's tabby fish face staring at us.

'There must be another way in!' said Anemone excitedly. 'Come on – let's go up and see!' She stood up, gave a great lash of her fishy tail, and before I could blink she had swum up to the cave entrance and disappeared inside.

After a moment she peered out. 'Come *on*, Rosie. Stop

hanging around!' she shouted down. But how the heck was I going to get up *there*?

'I can't fly!' I protested. 'Can't you *carry* me up?'

'You're far too heavy. You'll have to *swim* up, you idiot,' she shouted down impatiently. 'Flap your arms!'

I tried. I flapped my arms up and down and jumped. But nothing happened. I just stayed there. 'I *can't*!' I yelled back. 'It doesn't work!'

'Helpless human!' shouted Anemone. 'Hang on a minute then . . .'

Her head disappeared from the cave entrance and I waited. Cocklepuss peered down at me, burbling and mewing. Then Anemone's face reappeared beside him. 'There's some long seaweed coiled up in a corner here,' she cried out. 'Hang on – I'll chuck it down.'

A long rope of seaweed came snaking down through the air and slapped against the rocky side of the cliff. It came to rest just out of reach, a metre or so above my outstretched arms.

'Can't reach it!' I puffed, jumping up and down. 'I'm not tall enough!'

There was an exasperated 'Eugh!' sound from above. Then I heard Anemone's voice again, 'Stand on these then!' Several huge balls of tangled wet seaweed came hurtling down from above, nearly hitting me on the head.

'Watch out!' I yelled crossly. 'Are you trying to smother me?' There was a peal of laughter then, as I piled the dripping seaweed balls on top of one another and tried to clamber up them. They were really squashy, and I sank down into them.

I still couldn't *quite* reach. 'One more!' I shouted. Another huge ball of seaweed promptly flew down, knocking me off my pile and covering me in revolting slime.

'You're doing it on purpose!' I yelled angrily, picking myself up and piling all the seaweed into a slithery heap again. Anemone didn't reply, but I could hear her smug laughter from above. 'Just wait until I get up there!' I shouted.

I could *just* reach the seaweed rope now, and I began to haul myself up. It kept bending out of the way as I clambered up. And to make matters worse my hands and feet kept slipping because it was made of wet seaweed.

I was really cross and red in the face with the effort of climbing the rope by the time I reached the cave mouth. Several times I'd nearly fallen off, and only managed to steady myself by grabbing hold of cracks in the rock face.

Of course Anemone was just lying there in the mouth of the cave doing nothing to help me at all, with her tail all sparkly and rainbow-coloured in the sunshine. She looked as if she'd had a good rest while I was struggling.

She must have felt a bit guilty looking at my cross face and all the bits of slimy seaweed sticking to me. 'Sorry, Rosie,' she said, a bit more kindly. 'I'm just not used to humans. I forgot you can't swim properly.'

I realised this was a kind of apology. 'That's OK,' I said. 'I guess we just have to try and be friends the best we can.'

Anemone smiled and her pointed little teeth glinted.

'I'm really glad you rescued me, Rosie. Thank you. It's good having a human friend – I always thought all humans were totally hopeless before I met you.'

I felt a bit embarrassed now she was being nice to me. So I just smiled at her and then I peered into the back of the cave. I could see there were three dark tunnel entrances ahead of us. 'Which way now?' I asked.

But Cocklepuss chose for us before Anemone could reply. Without any hesitation at all he went to the middle entrance and disappeared into the darkness.

'Come on then,' I said. 'We'd better follow.'

Chapter Twenty-three
A Giant Problem

The tunnel went on for what seemed like ages, twisting and turning like a labyrinth, with side tunnels running off here and there and menacing cave entrances that loomed up at us out of the dark. If it hadn't been for more glow lights swarming over the walls to light our way, we'd have been in pitch darkness again.

I began to be afraid of what would happen if we lost Cocklepuss, or the glow lights decided to go out or all slither away into cracks in the walls. Anemone must have felt the same.

'Do you think he's taking us the right way?' she whispered in a small, scared voice. 'I don't like dark tunnels, and there's a whole network of them running from under the palace!'

I was scared too when she said that, but then I remembered that I was a pirate. 'Oh pirates are always doing this sort of thing,' I said airily. 'They hide their kegs of rum and stuff in smugglers' tunnels. Just wait until I tell my friends Cal and Plum about this – they'll be green with envy!'

'Talking of green – have you seen your hands and face lately?' Anemone asked.

I glanced down at my hands and saw that they were all green. It was horrible – it looked like I was going off or something. I rubbed them together and they felt revolting – all slippery and slimy. 'Is my face green too?' I gasped. 'What's going on? What is it?'

'It must be the slime off the tunnel walls.' Anemone pointed and sure enough I could see that the walls and floor of the tunnel were growing greener and greener the deeper in we went. I looked at Anemone's face, but of course it didn't really show on her. She was green anyway.

'We must be near the Cave of Slime,' I said. Just then Cocklepuss let out a low warning growl and crouched down as if he was hunting something. We had reached a place where the tunnel went round a bend and we couldn't see what lay beyond.

Anemone and I both stopped and held our breath. There was a scrabbling, scratchy noise going on around the bend of the tunnel. Suddenly a shadow was cast on the wall beside Anemone. I almost screamed. It was the shadow of a huge claw.

'Quick! The bag of fish! Get it ready!' screamed Anemone, just as something straight out of a nightmare came lurching around the corner. Cocklepuss took one look and fled, his fur bristling.

I didn't blame him. It was an enormous bright orange crab, as tall as a man. And it was scuttling along sideways towards us.

It stopped just in front of us and we didn't dare move a muscle. It waved its enormous pincers and edged slowly closer. It seemed to be sniffing the air, its horrid eyes waving on the ends of stalks like nightmare knitting needles.

'The fish! Throw it back where we came along!' yelled Anemone. For a moment I was paralysed with fear and then I managed slowly to untie the leather bag. A dank waft of appalling smell came out and the crab scrunched so close to me I could almost reach out and touch its damp shell.

I pulled out a piece of fish, waved it under where I hoped the crab's nose would be and then flung it, along with the leather bag, away down the tunnel. The crab hesitated for a moment and then scuttled after it.

'Quick! There's no time to lose!' I yelled, and I dashed around the corner with my heart pounding, closely followed by Anemone. There was the massive black door that I had seen in the scrying bubble, complete with the lock shaped like an oyster shell.

'It's the Cave of Slime! We've found it!'

'But how do we get in?' said Anemone faintly. 'The fishy stuff won't last that crab very long!'

I didn't really know what to do, but I had to do *something*. I went up to the lock and examined it closely. It was really strange – there didn't seem to be a keyhole in it. Just a tiny round hole at the top.

'How on earth do you unlock it?' I asked.'

Anemone came over and looked too. 'I've absolutely no idea,' she said, as if it was *my* fault. 'What do you suggest now, Miss Pirate?'

For a moment I was cross again, but when I looked at her face I realised she was being grumpy just to cover up how scared and disappointed she was feeling.

I reached over and took her hand. It felt damp and chilly. 'Don't worry. We'll find a way, Anemone. We'll get Yan Eye out – we haven't come this far for nothing.'

But I had to admit I was stumped. Not only that – I was worried about that horrid crab finishing up all the smelly fish and returning to start on *us*. Anemone slumped down, her back to the slimy wall, her head in her hands. 'Oh, what's the use?' she wailed. 'We've come all this way and we're not going to be able to get *in*.'

But I was thinking hard. What on earth would fit into that neat little round hole on top of the oyster shell? There must be *some* way to open the lock.

Then suddenly a thought floated into my head. The lock was an oyster. What do you find inside oysters?

Pearls.

It was worth a try. Quickly I rummaged in the pocket of my jeans and took out the tear of pearl. It lay in the palm of my hand glowing faintly in the pale green light of the glow lights.

I picked the tear up between finger and thumb and carefully dropped it into the little hole. It fitted perfectly and we heard a soft *clunk*, as if a well-oiled mechanism had just moved inside the lock.

Anemone just gaped at me and I gave her a triumphant grin and a thumbs up. 'Not so stupid a human after all, eh?'

'Wow, Rosie!' she said. 'That was really *clever!*'

We managed to turn the huge iron handle then and the door swung open with an ominous creak like a door in a haunted house. A horrid dank waft of stale air rushed out and we were looking into the Cave of Slime.

It was absolutely vile. The walls ran with slime, in great gouts of sickly green and blue and purple. Slime hung in blobs from the ceiling and dripped into gooey puddles on the floor. And all amongst the slime were things that I tried not to think about, things that looked horribly like skulls and bones in jumbled heaps.

There was a faint movement and there, huddled against the far wall, was Yan Eye, with a look of terror on his face.

Then I noticed that Anemone was staring at Yan Eye like she'd seen a ghost. And he was staring right back at her. They were so fixed in staring at one another in fact that they looked as if the air between them might tear apart.

Chapter Twenty-four

Yeuk!

The next bit is the slushy part and I would miss it out if I could, because it's so gross. But then you wouldn't know what happened.

Anemone floated over to Yan Eye sobbing and saying, 'Oh Flodraval, my love.' And Yan Eye was actually *crying* and holding his arms out towards Anemone. She fell into his arms and they clung to each other. It was totally puke-making.

Then there was lots of stuff like him saying, 'I never dared try to tell you who I really was,' and her saying, 'Oh Flodraval!' – in a soppy voice – 'I never knew it was you. I couldn't *believe* it.' And him saying, 'Oh my beloved.' Yes *really*. It was dead corny.

And this went on for about three minutes until I cleared my throat and said, 'Er . . . I hate to break this up but like, er, that crab's gonna come *back* any minute now . . .'

They both looked up in horror then. It was as if they'd totally forgotten that I was there and that they were in the Cave of Slime and all that life-threatening stuff. There was a silence and a smell of rotting gunge and I could hear water dripping.

Then, thank goodness, Yan Eye suddenly got grown up and sensible again. He pushed Anemone off his knee, stood up and strode towards the door. Then he poked his head out into the tunnel. He didn't speak, but his face was back to its normal grim faraway expression. To be honest, I preferred him that way.

Slowly he beckoned to us to come to the door and then he pointed up the tunnel, away from the direction of the crab. I could still hear it along there in the dark, scraping and rustling. There was a horrid kind of nibbling noise as well, that I didn't want to think about too much.

We nodded dumbly and followed Yan Eye out of the door. Luckily the glow lights were still swarming ahead of us, lighting the way with their dim green lanterns. The tunnel ahead began to twist and turn as it had before, until I wasn't at all sure which direction we were heading in.

We seemed to walk for ages and ages and my legs were beginning to ache. I began to feel very worried – there could be Finmen lurking around and I didn't fancy getting captured again and shoved into the Cave of Slime. I didn't have the tear of pearl any more and, anyway, how could I undo the lock from the inside?

'Don't worry,' said Yan Eye. 'I grew up in the palace, so

I know all these tunnels well. There's a way we might just be able to escape, but it's very risky. We might get captured again.'

I was amazed – that was the longest sentence I'd ever heard him speak! I made sure to stick close behind him because I could hear odd rustling noises in shadowy corners and always the sound of water dripping hollowly far away.

I wondered if we were being followed by something nasty, and a moment later my fears came true when I heard the distinct flap and squish of many Finmen feet running towards us along the tunnel up ahead.

Yan Eye must have heard it too, because he pointed urgently to a dark opening that loomed up on our left. It was pitch black and I didn't fancy going in there, but what else could we do?

We all crowded into the side opening and huddled together in the dark. I could smell Yan Eye's greasy cap and the fishy scales on Anemone's tail and I had this creepy feeling that we were being watched by unseen eyes in the darkness.

I hardly dared breathe as the squishing and flapping drew nearer. If they found us, there would be no escaping. Luckily, the Finmen all ran past the entrance to our hiding place. There were five of them and they all wore their grey cloaks with the hoods pulled up, making them look like ghosts in the half light. But they squelched right past us.

Shortly after the Finmen were safely past, the glow lights seemed to sense us and again began to swarm into our hidey hole – it was almost as if they had waited until the danger was past. I could see then that we were in a small cave with no other way in or out. I felt happier now that I could see. That is until Anemone tugged at my sleeve and pointed. I looked behind me at where she was pointing and suddenly saw an enormous craggy, rocky face gazing at us from the back wall of the cave. It was ghastly. It had dark, slitted eyes and a wide mouth that was all jumbled and jaggly, like it was made of a natural crack running across the rock.

But it wasn't just a crack in the rock, because as I looked it began to widen into a smile. I was petrified. I was sure it was going to open up and swallow us into its rocky self and that would be an end of us all and we'd be found as fossils ten million years on by a team of archaeologists.

It didn't though. To my surprise it spoke, in a creaking, rumbling voice. 'Greetings, Prince Flodraval, and welcome.'

Yan Eye swept off his cap and bowed low. 'Greetings, Cave Spirit,' he replied. 'It's many years since I have paid you a visit.'

The Cave Spirit chuckled in a grating sort of way. 'Not in my years. It is just the blink of an eyelid since I saw you last. What brings you into my underground kingdom today?'

'We're trying to find our way out to the daylight,' said Anemone. 'We're completely lost, so we'd be very glad if you could show us the way to go.'

'I can do better than that, little mermaid,' replied the Cave Spirit in a slow, fat kindly voice. And with that it began to open its mouth wider and wider.

There was a creaking, splintering noise, like a very large, old dungeon door slowly opening. The mouth opened further and further until it seemed as if the Cave Spirit's whole face must surely split apart.

Then I gasped in surprise, for I could see a steep set of rocky steps where the Cave Spirit's throat should be. It obviously intended us to go up them.

'Thank you, Cave Spirit. I shall bring you an offering of crystals,' said Yan Eye, pushing Anemone and me gently forward. I went first and it was a bit scary, but I could hear Anemone and Yan Eye following on behind me, and the glow lights flowed all over the walls to light our way.

The steps were so steep and narrow that I had to cling to the walls to haul myself up them. Eventually I got to a step that was a metre high and I had to look for a toehold to climb up it.

Yan Eye with his long legs, and Anemone with her creepy way of floating around, reached the top of the steps more easily. There we could see a wooden trap door, showing a crack of light from above.

Yan Eye gave a mighty heave and pushed open the door. It fell back with a hollow boom, and he sprang up into the place above with a sudden movement that seemed much too agile for an Old Git.

Anemone floated up after him and then Yan Eye reached down to help me through. I scrambled up and Yan Eye turned away – and before I knew it he and Anemone were at it again, in each other's arms! I felt really embarrassed and looked away not knowing what to do or say.

It was then, looking around, that I suddenly realised where we had emerged from the tunnel. We were in the throne room of the Fin King's palace.

Chapter Twenty-five

Nowhere to Run

Luckily there didn't seem to be anyone in the throne room at the moment. I grabbed Yan Eye's sleeve and shook his arm. 'I think we'd better get out of here, before someone finds us!' I said urgently.

Yan Eye just laughed. 'It's OK – I know a quick way out! Follow me!'

He bent over to put the trap door back in place and then, taking Anemone by the hand, he led her towards a low door at the back of the throne room that I hadn't seen before. It must have been hidden behind the pile of treasure. Yan Eye had to duck down to go through it.

I followed them and found myself in a corridor that was so narrow Yan Eye and Anemone had to go single file. It snaked around like the inside of a snail shell until I felt quite dizzy and lost my sense of direction completely.

The floor was rough and unworn – it looked as if

nobody came this way any more. After a couple of minutes we came to another low doorway, bolted on the inside. Yan Eye signalled for us to be quiet and then he carefully unbolted it and stepped through, looking around cautiously and beckoning us to follow.

It took me a moment to realise where we were. We were back outside the palace, standing just to one side of the driftwood gates.

In front of us was an open square, where market stalls were set up in rows. The place was a hive of activity, with Finmen milling around all over the place.

They weren't guards though, I realised with relief – none of them wore the beautiful gold and green tunics or the dolphin emblem. They were dressed in dull clothes in dark green and brown colours of seaweed and sand. None of them seemed to notice us – they were all far too busy with buying and selling.

The stalls were selling every imaginable kind of fish, and shells of all shapes and sizes – mussels, cockles, clams and covins, all piled up in dripping wet heaps. Some of the shellfish were escaping, gliding away down the legs of the stalls.

Each stall was in the charge of a morose Finwife, or a Finman with his woollen hood pulled up to hide his dismal face. The narrow, winding cobbled streets that I remembered dimly from my dream-like arrival at the palace led away from us on every side. Finchildren played in the shadows where the tall tumbledown houses crowded together.

I watched a wooden cart lumber past, pulled by two small mer-horses. It was heavily loaded with bright green seaweed. Then, to my horror, I noticed that dark shapes carrying spears were moving along one of the alleyways towards us. 'Look out!' I shouted, tugging at Yan Eye's sleeve. 'Finmen guards coming!' I could see there were three of them, moving rapidly our way.

I was too late. They had spotted us and, before we could run away or hide, one of them lifted one of those long horns to his lips and the unearthly note rang out loud and clear. Then they began to run towards us. Other Finfolk looked up from their work and began to point at us and jabber excitedly to one another.

Yan Eye looked wildly around him, but he didn't attempt to escape, because there, coming down a wider street to our left, we could see the Fin King's chariot racing towards us.

Before we knew it, in fact even faster than seemed possible, the chariot drew up on the cobbles beside us in the centre of the square with a horrible scrunching judder.

Yan Eye and I just stood there, frozen to the spot. But Anemone went all pale and see-through, and then she vanished. The Finmen guards ran up and yanked Yan Eye's arms behind his back before he could try to run.

Handing the horses' reins to a nearby Finman, the Fin King leaped down from the chariot and stood in front of us. He looked scarily furious, standing there holding his coiled whip in his right hand, all green and glistening.

The horrible mer-horses champed their golden bits and rolled their red eyes. The eyes reminded me of beach pebbles – dark and opaque. You couldn't tell if they were really looking at you or not.

But the Fin King was *definitely* looking at me. He seemed to ignore Yan Eye. I noticed Bordin's Band then, gleaming bright gold amongst his shining hair. He was still in its evil grip.

'How dare you break the enchantment of the Cave of Slime?' he bellowed.

'Enchantment . . . I . . . What do you mean?' All I had done was to let Yan Eye out. In any case – how did he know that it was me?

'How did you come by the tear that would open the lock?' he stormed, glaring at me with his green glassy eyes. 'And who *are* you? Are you a witch-child?'

'I . . . I'm just Rosie . . .' I stammered.

I looked away from the Fin King, not knowing what else to say. But I soon wished I hadn't – I nearly screamed in terror then at what I saw.

Loads of Finmen were coming from all directions, leaving their dank fish stalls and slinking over towards us to see what was going on. Even more of them were stepping out of dark doorways and gliding out of the narrow alleyways.

Finwives were appearing too, everywhere, trundling along slowly towards us, trailing their dank skirts on the wet cobbles. There were hundreds of them, all silent and grey.

The Finmen and their wives were gradually forming a

circle around us. I could smell their fishy breath and their damp clothes. It really gave me the creeps. There was no escape now unless I really used my wits.

Finchildren were there too – I could see them peeping out shyly from behind their mothers' skirts, their eyes glinting with curiosity. One of them pointed at me rudely with a webbed hand. 'What's that, Mama?' he asked.

'It's a human child,' she replied in a slow, gravelly voice. 'Hold my hand – it's dangerous.'

Me? Dangerous? I nearly laughed at that idea. But the Fin King soon scared the laughter right out of me.

'Answer me! Why did you break the enchantment?' he demanded in a voice as cold as ice.

'We . . . I . . . was rescuing Yan Eye . . . I mean Flod—'

The Fin King interrupted me before I could speak Yan Eye's true name. He laughed. A hollow, sarcastic laugh. 'And who pray *is* this *Yan Eye* – that he is worth risking your life for?' he said, poking at Yan Eye with the end of his whip.

Yan Eye had been struggling, trying to get away from the Finmen who were holding his arms. 'I am your brother – Flodraval!' he yelled angrily. 'Why do you deny it, you treacherous, mud-dwelling lump sucker!'

I got mad then as well. The pirate bit of me somehow welled up suddenly inside me and burst out and overflowed. 'He's your *twin*!' I shouted angrily. 'Can't you *see*?'

All of a sudden the Fin King seemed to deflate, like a burst balloon and he stopped poking Yan Eye. A weird faraway look came over his face so that he looked sad now, rather than angry. 'Twin?' he said, staring at me. 'Who told you that I had a twin?'

I shrugged. 'I just know.' I didn't want to mention Ginny Greenteeth.

The Fin King pulled a sneery sort of face. 'I *did* have a twin once,' he said, 'but that was long ago. Long before your small human lifetime. This disgusting old mortal is not my *twin*. Use your eyes! My twin was a Fin prince, beautiful as a wave of the sea. And he is lost to me.'

Yan Eye struggled even harder, but it was no use. His thin old man's body was too weak to escape from the grip of the two strong Finmen who held him. He spat on the ground in fury. 'Why do you still deny me, Haldor? Have you no shame for the evil that you did?'

But the Fin King looked at Yan Eye as if he was something Cocklepuss had dragged out of a rubbish bin. 'You are no Finman,' he said in a superior voice. 'You are merely a revolting mortal! Look at your wrinkled brown skin.' He seemed to shudder in disgust and he turned away from Yan Eye.

I knew that I had to make him see it all somehow. How Yan Eye had aged and lost his Finman looks because he'd had to go and live amongst humans when he was cursed and thrown out of Hildaland. How could I prove it to him? It seemed hopeless. But I had to try *something*.

'You had a duel, didn't you?' I said suddenly, just to keep him remembering the past. 'That's when your brother lost his eye!'

The Fin King glared at me. 'This mortal has only one eye like my brother, it is true. But that could happen to anyone!' Weirdly though, he faltered then and looked as if he might be going to burst into tears at any moment.

Then he seemed to revert to his angry self. He shook himself like a bird fluffing out its feathers, and the fins rippled and gleamed gold along the underside of his arms. His glittering green eyes lit up and he cracked the seaweed whip in rage.

'Nobody argues with the Fin King!' he yelled. 'Nobody trespasses in my kingdom and gets away with it! You will both be taken to the Cave of Slime to await your punishment!'

It was so scary that I felt frozen to the spot like a block of ice. Only my eyes seemed to be able to move and I stared at Bordin's Band, clamped tight around the Fin King's head. It seemed to be glowing with its own strange power, as if it was *feeding* – sinking its horrid tendrils deep into the Fin King's anger. I felt hopeless all of a sudden. What on earth could I possibly do to fight against such strong magic?

Chapter Twenty-six

Quick Thinking!

An evil wind gusted all around us, sending dark torn clouds racing across the sky and making the Finwives shiver and gather in their skirts. The terrifying mer-horses snorted white spray from their nostrils and stamped their forefeet uneasily on the cobbles.

The crowd of Finfolk around us started shuffling and murmuring and then this horrible sound began. They were moaning, singing low under their breath, and the sound swelled slowly and began to rise into an eerie despairing chant. It was as if they were building up power against us.

I went all wobbly. I absolutely shook with fear. The Fin King looked about five metres tall and the dark clouds seemed as if they might swoop down on me like carrion birds. I was so scared I felt myself go all frilly round the edges.

I heard Anemone's voice then, inside my head. 'You just

let yourself go all frilly round the edges . . . and then you imagine yourself slowly fading away . . .'

I tried then, really hard, to make myself go see-through. I closed my eyes and squeezed my body together, trying to make it smaller. Trying to imagine myself slowly fading away. But it didn't work.

I opened my eyes and the Fin King was still there, glaring down at me with his eyes like green agates. I tried to run, but my legs were like bendy sausages and they wouldn't work at all. I looked across desperately at Yan Eye, but his head was slumped down on his chest in despair and he might have been turned to stone for all the use he was being. Maybe his old man strength had finally given out on him.

I felt strong arms wrench my hands behind my back and I was pushed forwards. It was then that a voice spoke suddenly between Yan Eye and me. It really made me jump.

'It's true what she says. You have given in to evil. And you *did* have a duel – with your own brother.'

It was Anemone. She was appearing slowly, hovering by my side, shimmering and gleaming in the sunlight. I saw how beautiful she was then, in a weird, fishy unearthly kind of way.

The Fin King's eyes nearly popped out of his head. 'Anemone!' he gasped. The crowd of Finfolk stopped chanting suddenly, all at once. They stood still staring at us and then a different kind of murmur began to spread amongst them. I thought I heard the words 'Princess Anemone' being whispered, and there was excitement in their voices now, rather than anger.

The Fin King stopped looking furious abruptly, like someone flicking a light switch. He went all cringing and smiley instead. 'Anemone, my love . . .' he moaned, stretching out his hand towards her. It was revolting. Like he was sucking up to her in a really gross way.

'Pah!' Anemone spat angrily at his feet. 'I was never your love and you know it! You were in love with power!'

The Fin King looked at her and his stony eyes grew wide. He looked as if he might swoop on her and kill her at any moment. But she stood her ground and carried on bravely. 'This poor old man is your brother Flodraval! *He* was the one who loved me. You banished him and cursed him and all of Hildaland with your evil enchantment.'

Another low murmur ran through the gathered crowd of Finfolk.

'Is it true?' they were saying.

'Our own king? *He* laid the curse on our people? He would do *that* to us?' Some of them were beginning to look angry. Then a voice shouted from the back of the crowd. 'It must be true! Princess Anemone would never lie!'

Another voice answered the first. 'He cursed us!'

Then a third yelled, 'Aye. And he banished his own brother!'

'He's kept us all in thrall long enough!' shouted another.

'Tribute. Tribute and treasure! That's all he ever thinks of. He never thinks of *us*, wretched and poor as we are!' stormed another voice. And then more and more Finfolk began to raise their voices in anger until the whole crowd began to buzz like a swarm of angry bees. The Fin King stood there helpless, watching his people rising up against him.

'You see!' cried Yan Eye victoriously. 'Our people know the truth now!'

The Fin King seemed to go all limp then and he dropped his seaweedy whip and slumped to the ground. He stared down in shame and his glittering fins grew dull and lifeless.

At last he looked up at Anemone and began to speak slowly: 'An evil enchantment. It *is* true. It's all my fault and I have made my own people suffer, because I gave in to dark magic.' And with those words the Fin King began to cry. Great slow tears began to run down his face and soak into his beautiful golden beard. It was terrible. I didn't know where to look.

Anemone was gazing intently at Yan Eye now, as if he might vanish away in front of her at any moment. And Yan Eye stood still as a stone and kept his one eye fixed on her like a staring marble.

'Show him your gills, Flodraval,' she hissed. 'Then he cannot deny it's you any longer!' The crowd of Finfolk all stood still too and gazed in expectation. Nobody said a word.

Then the Finmen guards released their grip on Yan Eye and me. He raised his hand and slowly unwound the red scarf from around his neck. A gasp went up from the crowd as everyone could see his gills at last. 'A Finman! He is a Finman . . . It is our Prince Flodraval . . .' They all began to mutter excitedly.

The Fin King stared blankly at Yan Eye as if he couldn't believe what he saw. Then he spoke slowly, in a cracked voice, '*You.* It *is* you, Flodraval!'

Yan Eye looked at his brother gravely. 'Aye, Haldor, and our people know now what you have done to me.'

'Your fins . . .' stuttered the Fin King, 'your shining skin and your beautiful hair . . .'

'All withered and gone. I am more human than Finman now, thanks to your banishing me,' replied Yan Eye sadly.

The Fin King stood up then, tall and proud in front of them all, and raised his hands to the crowd. 'I am truly sorry for what I have done,' he shouted. And in that moment I could see that part of him was still noble, despite the evil power of the band that still shone amongst his golden curls.

'I demanded that people bring me gold and precious jewels,' he continued. 'If they had nothing to offer I threw them into the Cave of Slime. And I was so angry and jealous that Anemone was to marry Flodraval, making him wealthy beyond my wildest dreams, that I banished him and cursed all my people!'

There was a loud roar of fury from the crowd now, but the Fin King raised his hands for silence.

'Let him speak,' came a cry from the back, in the hollow drawl of a Finwife.

The Fin King nodded. 'I wished no girls should be born,' he went on, 'and that all the Finwives would grow depressed and miserable . . . I wished it and this evil gold band made it so!' He raised his hands to wrench hopelessly at Bordin's Band as he spoke.

One of the Finmen, a small one with silver fins and a thin cross face, pushed to the front of the crowd and spoke loudly, 'If all this is true, Sire, then how are you going to make amends?' And other voices began to join in. 'Yes, he must make amends!' 'He must lift the terrible curse he has placed upon us!'

'I know I should do that now. I know it!' Haldor wept. 'But what should I do? I cannot get this devilish thing from my head!' He still struggled with the gold band as he spoke – and he was looking straight at *me* again.

Why was he looking at me? Did he still think I had magical powers? What on earth was I supposed to say to sort out all this mess? I mean – I'm just a little kid. It was *unreal* – suddenly all the Finmen and Finwives and the little Finchildren and *everyone* – they were all looking at me, waiting for an answer. Even Yan Eye and Anemone.

Then, at that moment, I felt really proud – like being Anne Bonny only even better, because I was just *me*. There I was, just being my ordinary self – and people were taking notice. People don't usually, because I'm the youngest in our family. It was scary, but really good in a way!

All at once, I remembered what Old Plum had said, back on the harbour at home, when the Old Gits were telling us their yarns. It seemed so long ago, like another lifetime – so much had happened since then that up until that instant I had completely forgotten it. Maybe there *was* a way to get the evil band off!

'I know what you should do,' I said firmly. 'Give away *everything* that you own – all that treasure you've got stashed away!'

A roar went up from the crowd of Finfolk. 'Yes! Give us back our gold and jewels. Give back what is rightfully ours!'

'And . . .' I shouted, having another good idea suddenly, 'let Yan – I mean Flodraval – and Anemone get married. That might help weaken the power of the band too!'

Anemone gripped my arm tightly. 'What if it doesn't work?' she hissed in my ear.

I said nothing. I knew what she was thinking – she was worried she'd turn into a sad Finwife if she married Yan Eye. But I was waiting to see what the Fin King would say. The crowd fell silent again, waiting too. For a few moments he said nothing at all and then he nodded slowly.

'Yes,' he said, 'you are a wise child. I'd do anything to have my brother back. I've missed him so badly. All that treasure people brought – it all meant nothing to me in the end – I was so sad and lonely. And I see now I was wrong – Anemone loves Flodraval so much she would marry him even now, when he's so old.'

I looked at Yan Eye then and, to my disgust, I saw that he was crying again too! Yan Eye, the Old Git – *crying* in *public*! Tears were running down his cheek from his one eye. They were all at it! All the so-called grown-ups!

'Yes,' said Yan Eye in a choking voice, fiercely wiping his face with his sleeve, 'and I've never loved another all my life!'

The Fin King turned to Yan Eye and put his arms

around him. 'Flodraval,' he said solemnly, 'I welcome you home. I give you my throne willingly.' Then he turned to face the crowd of Finmen and Finwives who had gathered even closer to listen to what was going on.

'Open the royal treasure house!' he shouted. 'Empty the throne room of all its treasure too! I will give away all my wealth to you, my people, and release each and every one of you from the hardship you have suffered!'

A huge roar went up from the crowd and the Finfolk all began to hug one another and do little dances on the cobbles. And the Fin King began to smile. Only a tiny bit at first, but then this huge grin gradually spread right across his face.

Slowly he raised his hands to his head and grasped the band of gold. It shifted a little and he began to work it loose. There was an awed silence. Everyone was staring at him, waiting to see what would happen.

All of a sudden the Fin King threw back his head and laughed – a great bellowing, happy laugh that rang right across the square. And then he raised Bordin's Band from his head and held it high up in the air for all to see.

'The curse is broken!' he shouted. 'My people will no longer be the terror of the seas! Empty the treasure house! And lock this evil thing away in there, so it can harm no one!'

What happened then was amazing. The Finwives all began to shimmer and vibrate, as if somebody was shaking them very, very fast. Then you could see that they were plumping out and their sad faces were being smoothed, like someone smoothing a clean sheet when they put it on to a bed.

All around were cries of joy and surprise. Finwives were turning to their husbands as they saw what was happening to their friends – and their husbands were holding out their arms to hug their beautiful, plump, happy wives in delight.

Before long we were surrounded by smiling, happy people. Even the guards no longer looked grim and solemn. They were shining, pale green, and their faces were young and joyful.

Some of the women were human-shaped, with legs, like Flodraval and Haldor – beautiful young Finwives with iridescent fins, like the ones I had seen in the hunting scenes on the tapestries in the great hall. Others were mermaids like Anemone, floating above the ground like she did. Little children were gasping in surprise, seeing their mothers growing happy and beautiful before their eyes. Some of the smaller ones ran away to hide behind rocks – they couldn't understand what was happening and they were so used to seeing their mothers miserable.

Then I looked at Yan Eye. And that was the greatest surprise of all. He was rapidly growing younger before my very eyes. His wrinkles seemed to melt away. He tore off his greasy cap and his thin grey hair slowly turned to gold and shining curls, just like his brother's.

Soon he was as young and handsome as the Fin King. His skin was no longer brown and weather-beaten, but shone with the same faint green opalescence of all the

Finfolk. The only difference you could see between Yan Eye and the Fin King was that Yan Eye still had only his one eye.

He smiled at me then and my insides turned to jelly. He was even *more* handsome than his brother! He wasn't an Old Git any more at all – he'd gone into reverse. Even the missing eye just gave him an interesting pirate-like sort of look.

Anemone flew across to him and they just about fell into one another's arms. Everyone around set up a loud cheer then and the weeping Fin King mopped his eyes and his golden beard with the hem of his flowing cloak.

Yan Eye kissed Anemone, right on the mouth with everybody looking. It was dead embarrassing, but I sort of liked it too in a squirmy sort of way. Then he turned to his brother. 'I don't want your throne . . .' he said. 'To have Anemone back at last is enough.'

The Fin King smiled. 'Then we'll share the throne,' he said, 'just as we should always have done.'

He turned to the gathered crowd and shouted to them in a loud clear voice, 'Prepare a great feast. We must celebrate!'

Chapter Twenty-seven

A Banquet Fit for Kings

For the next few hours the whole palace was a hive of activity. The entire place was given a spring-clean until at last all the grotty old slime was gone. The huge banqueting hall was scrubbed and washed down with soft yellow sponges until it was spotless. Then the long tables were set for a massive feast, just like the ones shown on the tapestries.

The huge pile of jewels and gold from the throne room, plus all the stuff from the treasure house, was shared out between everyone. People carted it away by the bucket-load – it was like everyone winning the lottery all at once. The Finwives chattered excitedly. They dressed up in ropes of pearls and put shining coronets on their heads.

I was allowed to dress up too! Two beautiful young Finwives took me to a chamber up a wide, curving flight of stairs, where they had filled a huge, round tub with water. I stripped off my slimy clothes and plunged gratefully in. The water was bubbly and bright turquoise and in no time at all I felt calm and relaxed at last.

There was a bar of soap in the shape of a little round puffer fish, so I began to scrub the horrible slime off my arms and legs. The odd thing was though, no matter how hard I scrubbed at my skin, the green just didn't seem to want to come off. Maybe the water wasn't proper water – everything was strange in this land! In the end I just gave up.

The Finwives brought me a long flowing dress in swirling patterns of sea green and deep cobalt blue. When I looked at myself in the mirror I saw I was really beautiful, like Anemone, and I did a little twirl to see how my skirt flounced out in a circle around me. Doing girly things could be fun after all I realised – especially when a moment later they brought me a sparkly gold tiara, set with aquamarines, to put in my hair!

'There now, Rosie,' said one of the Finwives admiringly. 'You look just like a fairy tale princess!'

I laughed happily at this idea. What would Mum and Auntie Lyn think if they could see me now! But I was getting hungry by then, so I gathered up my long skirts and ran down the sweeping staircase to rejoin the bustle of preparations in the banqueting hall.

Page boys were scurrying everywhere with plates and knives and forks and stuff. The children were playing marbles with giant pearls and got under everyone's feet. And the Finmen were brandishing jewel-encrusted swords and gleaming daggers from the treasure house, swaggering around, laughing with their new weapons strapped to their belts.

By the time the feast was ready I was absolutely ravenous and very excited – it turned out that Anemone and I were to be the guests of honour! Haldor and Flodraval were seated opposite each other in the very centre of the long table, with Anemone next to Flodraval and me next to Haldor.

Flodraval wanted all of his people to join in the celebrations, but of course not everyone could be seated in the banqueting hall. So the page boys were kept very busy running to and fro to those outside, with plates and bowls piled high with food.

I recognised some of those seated at the table as Finmen who had been in the throne room when Yan Eye and I first arrived. They must be some of the top people in the Fin court I decided. They were not miserable any more, but smiling and happy, raising their glasses in endless toasts. I stuffed myself until I was just about bursting. It was a good job I love seafood!

Great piles of seaweed were mounded into enormous bowls, and people brought in fish of every size and shape that ever swam in the sea. There was fisherman's pie, fish risotto, crab sandwiches, great dishes full of prawns, and in the centre the most enormous lobster I had ever seen, decorated with pink coral strands.

I smothered a burp and turned to Anemone, who was

sitting opposite me. She was just raising a silver goblet to offer Haldor a toast. 'That was the best feast I've ever had,' I said. 'I couldn't eat another prawn!'

Anemone gave a horrified gasp. 'Rosie, you must go home!' she yelled urgently. 'You've been here too long . . . and you have eaten Finfolk food!' She looked really scared all of a sudden.

'What do you mean?' I said. I was really enjoying myself. I felt happy amongst the smiling Finfolk, and the weird dreamy feeling that had hovered around me when I first arrived in Hildaland had gone completely. I must have got used to being there, I realised. But maybe this was not such a good thing after all – Anemone was already pushing me to get up out of my seat. 'Quick. You can't eat any more Finfood – it's changing your body! You mustn't stay a moment longer!' she exclaimed. 'You're getting *really green*!'

Chapter Twenty-eight

Panic Stations!

I'd totally forgotten about going green with all that had been happening with the banquet. I looked down at my hands. To my horror they were absolutely bright green now! Anxiously I peered at my face in the side of the silver goblet I had been drinking from. It was true – I was an interesting shade of green all over. I really freaked out. What was going on?

Anemone turned to Haldor. 'Send for the chariot quickly!' she yelled. 'We must get Rosie to the sea before it's too late!' Haldor took one look at me and a horrified look came over his face. He leaped to his feet and rushed out of the door, bellowing for someone to fetch the chariot quickly.

Anemone rushed me to the door and Yan Eye was beside her all of a sudden, helping to hurry me along. 'Humans can't stay in Hildaland for long,' he panted, pushing me along the corridor.

'But . . . why?' I asked again, desperate now as we reached the palace gates and the mer-horse chariot drew up with a great rumble and clatter, striking up sparks from the cobbles. I didn't want to leave yet and miss the excitement that was yet to come – there were going to be minstrels and jugglers and fireworks. 'I *want* to stay!' I protested.

But they bundled me into the chariot and then we were off at a breakneck speed, Yan Eye and Anemone and me. We went so fast that all the breath was knocked out of me and I couldn't speak again or ask what was going on.

The landscape flashed past with a blur of cobbled streets and alleyways and red fields full of anemones and black and white mer-cows all jumbled up. Before I knew it we scrunched to a halt.

We were down on the shore and there was Yan Eye's little boat, *Hildaland*, abandoned at the edge of the water just as if none of the whole adventure had happened at all.

Yan Eye and Anemone literally lifted me out of the chariot and placed me into the boat. Yan Eye began to shove it hard, to get it off the shingle. I found my breath at last and asked again, despairingly, 'But *why* – why can't I stay? I don't want to miss all the fun!'

'You *can*, Rosie,' replied Anemone, floating now in the water beside the boat. 'I would love for you to stay – we will always be friends now. But if you stay any longer and eat any more of our food, you'll have to stay for ever! See how green you've got – you're beginning to turn into a Fingirl!'

I looked down at my hands again in horror. Was that

webbing beginning to form between my fingers?

'Do you *want* to stay, Rosie? We can be like sisters and live at the palace,' said Anemone hopefully. I looked at her doubtfully and her face looked sad all of a sudden. She was really going to miss me I realised. But . . . there was Mum, and Dad, and fish and chips . . . and the Harbour Gang . . .

'I can't . . . I . . . I don't belong here. I have to go home,' I said. My voice sounded small and echoey and sad. I was going to miss Anemone too I realised, as a big lump formed in my throat. I looked down then at my beautiful long dress with its swirling patterns and saw that it was beginning to fade away before my eyes. My own normal clothes were coming back, somehow magically cleaned of all the green slime.

'You can get home if you try hard!' said Yan Eye. 'You still have human energy about you. But we haven't a moment to lose. Just close your eyes now and keep them tight shut!' he ordered sternly. I felt ever so scared then all of a sudden, and quickly did as he said, sobbing with fear. I really *didn't* want to turn into a Fingirl and have to stay in Hildaland for ever!

'But Anemone – will I see you again?' I asked, hearing her sploshing in the water next to the boat, but not daring to look. I didn't want to leave her either – she was my best friend now, after all we'd been through together.

'Of course. We're friends for ever! But go! Go *now*!'

'How do I row the boat? The oars are gone, remember!' I shouted anxiously.

'Just think of where you want to go!' shouted Yan Eye.

'Focus your mind!'

I briefly thought of home – Alex eating sausages in the kitchen. I opened my eyes then for a moment and to my surprise found that I was already a little way out from the shore.

Yan Eye was standing there at the edge of the water, staring at me. He looked really worried. 'Shut your eyes! Think about home!' he shouted.

But I thought about Hildaland. I thought about being stuck there, and never being able to see Mum and Dad and Alex again. The boat seemed to waver and then it began to move slowly back towards the shore.

'No!' shouted Yan Eye angrily. 'Think about home. Think about the Harbour Gang!'

I closed my eyes again and focussed desperately on Cal and Plum. Their faces swam up in front of my closed eyelids. After a few seconds I opened my eyes again and saw I was quite a way from the shore now. Anemone was at the edge, floating in the sea.

'But *how* shall I see you?' I shouted frantically.

'I'll come to you! After I've been home to see my family. I promise!' she shouted back across the water, her voice getting fainter. 'Now go!'

But the boat was moving back towards the shore again. I felt cold and afraid. Was I going to be stuck in Hildaland now for ever? Firmly I closed my eyes.

'Think about searching for covins!' yelled Yan Eye. 'Think about fishing in the harbour!'

I thought hard about home. I did it with all my might,

even though I wanted to open my eyes and look at Anemone and Yan Eye. The boat felt as if it was going round and round in circles. It was horrible and dizzy-making.

I opened my eyes to see how far I'd got and found that I was surrounded by mist. It lay all around me in a thick fog. There was no way of telling which way I was going, or which way was home.

'I'll come and find you!' came Anemone's voice, very faint and distant now.

And then Yan Eye's again. 'Think about Old Plum and Pordy!'

And then I was in a thick white silence and there was nothing but blank fog all around me. I don't know how long I drifted there. It was like a horrid nightmare.

I kept thinking about home as hard as I could. I thought of Old Plum with his wrinkled, chicken-skin neck. I thought about Pordy with his thick socks and his wellington boots. I even thought about all the old men propping up the bar at The Anchor pub.

I thought about Alex, and all the big boys, teasing me and not letting me join in their games. I thought about Cal – but that made me realise I *still* had nothing to show him for joining the Harbour Gang. Unless I stayed bright green of course – *that* would give him something to think about . . . The thought of this made me feel quite ill – the sooner I got away from Hildaland the better!

So I shut my eyes tightly and pretended to be Anne Bonny, setting a course for home in my pirate ship. I saw myself in my mind's eye, standing at the wheel, steering right into our own home harbour.

Only when I looked closely at the picture of me inside my head, I realised I was just plain ordinary old *me*. I didn't need to pretend to be Anne Bonny any more. Being myself was just fine.

Just then a whinnying bubble close by the boat interrupted my train of thought and opening my eyes I saw Ginny, mounted on Dulse. She no longer had weird bulging eyes and blotchy frog skin – she was a beautiful young woman, with long green hair and a face as clear and shining as spring water.

'Thank you, Rosie!' she shouted. 'Thank you for everything!' and she waved happily as she galloped swiftly away, getting fainter already through the mist.

'Wait, Ginny!' I yelled desperately, 'Where are you going?'

But I didn't really need a reply. I knew where she was going. She was heading towards Hildaland. Somehow I knew everything was going to be OK now between her and Haldor.

A huge wave of relief washed over me. Everything was coming right and I knew then I would soon be home too. And suddenly there was the harbour wall, looming up right above me! The real, solid, ordinary harbour wall. I was about to round it, right by the lighthouse.

Before I knew it there was a solid *bump*! And I was on West Beach, very near the seaweed bank where I had first found Anemone. The *Hildaland* scrunched up firmly on to the shingle and stopped rocking about.

For a few moments I sat there dazed, wondering how on

earth I had got home. Then something red caught my eye in the bottom of the boat and I bent down to look. It was a little, soggy, red bundle . . .

I picked it up and I realised what it was . . . 'Spider Sam! You're safe after all!' He was very wet and bedraggled though, with seaweed strands tangled all around his arms and legs.

But he was still patiently grinning his silky little smile. And there, wrapped around his waist, was Anemone's bracelet! Now how had that got there? Untwisting the bracelet from Spider Sam's waist, I fastened it around my own wrist. It felt good there – a reminder of my special friend.

Then I understood – of course! Anemone must have taken Spider Sam off my belt and wrapped her bracelet around him while we were rowing towards Hildaland. Maybe it was her way of leaving a little message of friendship for me. She must have known all along that we would have to part.

I felt a bit sad then, because I didn't know if I would ever see my friend again. I turned the bracelet on my wrist and admired the delicate little shells. It made me feel powerful, and I realised that meeting Anemone had given me another gift too – because I could enjoy wearing girly things now!

But I was a wild, free girl like Anemone, not the useless, helpless kind of girl Plum always tried to make me out to be. I'd rescued Anemone and helped the Finfolk to undo the curse that had hung over them for so long. And I'd *really* been to sea, out in a little boat on the choppy waves, all the way to a magical island – not like the boys!

Thinking of the boys made me realise suddenly that I was back home at last, but just sitting in the boat doing nothing. *Mum!* What *was* the time? She was going to absolutely *kill* me. I jumped hastily out of the boat and began to stagger up the shingle. Glancing down at my hands I saw to my relief that they were back to their normal colour – phew! Hurriedly I scrambled up the beach and began to run along the harbour side. I just left the *Hildaland* there, pulled up on the shingle.

I was really out of breath by the time I burst in at the back door. Mum was in the kitchen doing ironing. I could smell the familiar, toasty scorched smell of Dad's clean shirts hanging up to air.

'What time is it?' I gasped. 'Did I miss tea?'

Mum looked at me with a funny frown. 'Tea? Is that all you ever think about you kids – your empty tummies? Get away, it's only three!'

Three? How the heck could it be? I'd been away for *ages*. I looked up at the clock above the fridge to check. Sure enough it was dead on three.

'But . . .' My brain felt numb. 'What day is it?'

'Honestly,' said Alex, who was rinsing out a glass at the sink, 'Sunday. Still Sunday. You're mental.'

Mum banged the iron down and reached for another shirt.

It couldn't be still Sunday afternoon. And yet – it was as if no time had passed back home at all. It was weird. I felt a bit sick again.

'Are you OK?' asked Mum anxiously. 'Have some crisps if you're *that* hungry.'

My face must have looked pale or something. I hoped it didn't look green! 'No – no I'm fine. I'm just going up to my room,' I said awkwardly. I dodged away from Alex who was flapping me with a tea towel and dashed upstairs.

I propped Spider Sam in the sun on my windowsill to dry. Out of the window I could see Cal in the distance, sauntering along the harbour towards Sugar Tongue as if nothing unusual had happened at all.

Twiddling Anemone's bracelet on my wrist while I thought about what had happened, it suddenly came to me! I *had* found something No Man Has Found Before! I'd found a mermaid's bracelet, hadn't I? And it was real and solid – nobody could say it wasn't.

I whirled around and dashed downstairs and out the back door before anyone could say anything or ask me what I was doing. Then I ran as fast as I could towards Sugar Tongue, my breath bursting in my lungs. I had to catch up with Cal.

Chapter Twenty-nine

In the Harbour Gang at Last

Even Cal was impressed by the bracelet. I caught up with him and showed him it just as he reached Sugar Tongue. Plum was waiting at the meeting place: I could see his legs sticking out from behind the boy with the spyglass.

'Look what I found on the shore!' I gasped, struggling to catch my breath as I handed it to Cal. He took the bracelet and held it up to have a good look.

'Wow!' he said. 'That's awesome! Where did you find it?'

I hesitated. I didn't want to start the mermaid jokes up again. 'On West Beach,' I said. It was true after all – I *had* found it there to begin with – when it was on Anemone's wrist!

'How on earth was it made?' asked Cal. I could tell he was amazed.

'I don't know,' I replied truthfully. We both looked at the bracelet as Cal turned it in his fingers.

'It doesn't look humanly possible to thread anything as fine as that,' he said.

'No. Not humanly possible.' I smiled secretly to myself. Let them think mermaids didn't exist. I didn't care any more.

Plum thought the bracelet was really cool. 'Can I borrow it to show my sister?' he asked. But I didn't let him. I snatched it back and put it on my wrist. No way was I letting him take it.

'So that's it then!' said Cal suddenly. 'You're in the Gang now! You've found something No Man Has Ever Found Before.'

I sneered at this and looked Cal straight in the eye. 'A *man* still hasn't found it!' I said proudly. 'I'm a woman!'

Cal laughed and cuffed me on the back of my head. It hurt and tears came to my eyes, but I said nothing. I felt all warm and glowing inside me. The boys thought I was cool. I was a full member of the gang now. A real *living* Anne Bonny!

There was a huge fuss next day when people began to realise that Yan Eye was missing. Someone found the *Hildaland* pulled up on West Beach with the oars missing and everyone got all excited and put two and two together to make five. They assumed he'd got lost out at sea and drowned. They called out the police and a special diving team and people hunted for him for days – but they never found him of course.

Modern Marie Celeste – Old Sailor Vanishes, read the headlines in the local paper the next morning. *The* Hildaland, *a small boat belonging to Fred Morgan, was found deserted* . . .

In the end everyone gave up searching for Yan Eye and they had a sad little memorial service for him, down on the harbour. I didn't tell anyone what I knew. What would be the point? They would only have laughed at me. Only *I* knew that Yan Eye *had* died in a way and gone for ever – but in another way he was safe and happy. And that his name was Flodraval, not Fred Morgan. Only *I* knew he was a Finman.

The Old Git Gang looked sad now because there were only two of them. They still met up and sat in their usual place on the harbour wall every day. But they looked worried.

Every so often Old Plum would crane his wrinkled neck up and look anxiously behind him out to sea. Or Pordy would clear his throat with a deep rumble and stare down at his wellington boots glumly.

I knew what they were thinking. *Who's next?* They knew they were old and they missed their silent friend.

But one morning when I was watching them out of my bedroom window, an old man I didn't recognise was tottering up to them along the quayside. He was bent, like an old willow tree.

The Old Gits moved up a bit to make a space and he sat down beside them. I watched for a bit and I saw him begin to wave his arms as if he was talking. Then he held them out in front of him a metre apart, like an old fisherman showing the length of a huge, imaginary fish he had caught.

Old Plum and Pordy leaned backwards like they were laughing their heads off. I was afraid Pordy was going to overbalance into the dock he laughed so hard.

From that day on, there have been three Old Gits once more. So their gang has the right number. It feels good that way, and Old Plum and Pordy have cheered up again.

The new Old Git is called Noddy, because he always nods his head and mutters 'aye' under his breath as he walks along. But nobody knows where he came from. He's from away.

Mum was totally and utterly gobsmacked when I asked her if we could go to town next Saturday and get me some scrunchies for my hair.

'Red ones, not pink,' I added hurriedly when I saw the gleam in her eye. 'I want to grow my hair long,' I said, thinking of Anemone.

Mum gaped at me like a goldfish. She and Auntie Lyn had been trying to get me to do that for *ages*. But then her face fell. 'In a greasy pigtail I suppose,' she sighed, 'like pirates always have.'

I thought about this. 'No – I want a long ponytail,' I replied. 'And I want a new glittery green and blue top like Melissa's got,' I added, remembering my gorgeous dress from Hildaland.

Mum nearly swallowed her own head, her mouth opened that wide. She was speechless for once.

'Girly girly!' mocked Alex, pouting and doing a mincing movement with his hips.

'Shut up!' I hissed fiercely. 'I *am* a girl, you plonker!'

'I thought you were a pirate,' said Dad, looking up from the *Evening News and Star*. There was yet another article on the front about Yan Eye. *Where Did Mystery Stranger Hail From?* read the headline. They were still milking the story for all it was worth. If only they knew!

I stood up straight. 'Yes, I am – but I'm a female one! Like Anne Bonny was.'

Mum raised her eyes to the ceiling and sagged her shoulders. Her hopes of a ballet dancer or a model were dashed yet again. But Dad winked at me and chuckled. 'That's my Rosie!' he said.

I put Anemone's bracelet on my bedroom windowsill. Every day I look at it, just to remind me of my visit to the island of the Finfolk. One day Melissa came round for tea and she picked it up. 'Wow! This is really *cool*!' she said. 'I'm dead jealous – where did you buy it?'

'I didn't buy it. I kind of . . . *found* it . . .' I began. And then I told her the whole story, beginning with when I found Anemone on the shore. And she listened right the way through and do you know what?

She believed me!

So now Melissa's my best friend – apart from Anemone

of course. And she's waiting to do a test to join the Harbour Gang! We still keep the story of Hildaland a secret from the boys though. Partly because they would probably never believe us and partly because it's really fun having a secret from them. Sometimes we hint bits of it to them, but we won't tell them the whole thing. Nobody else in the human world knows the whole story, apart from me and Melissa.

For the next week or so you could still see Hildaland on the horizon. It just looked like a bank of cloud, so nobody really noticed it, or knew it was there, except me. It drifted slowly southwards and one day when I looked out of my window it had gone.

Spider Sam was back in his proper place, hanging from the bedrail. 'I wonder where the Finmen live in winter?' I whispered to him. I remembered Yan Eye saying that Hildaland was the summer isle of his people.

Maybe they go under the waves and live on the seabed, tucked up safe from the winter storms. That's when they would go hunting sharks, mounted on the huge sea horses like Tangle and Dulse.

I tried to imagine what it would be like, living down there in the watery world of the Finmen. But I still couldn't really understand it. What was water and what was air? What was it Anemone had said? *The air is water and the water's air and both are both at once.*

It just didn't make sense. But then neither did Hildaland. It was there, and it wasn't there. It was the island that wasn't there! 'When we meet Anemone again, maybe she can explain it to us,' I said, pulling Spider Sam down and propping him up beside me on the pillow.

I hope I *do* meet Anemone again some day. But I'm glad I decided to come home, rather than stay in Hildaland for ever. It's brilliant being a full member of the Harbour Gang. Specially now that there's another girl in it and we can gang up on the boys. It's really great having a special girl friend too – a human one – and sharing girls' secrets. Mind you, I still think the tap-dancing's naff. I guess part of me will always be a pirate.

If you enjoyed this book, try:

KUMARI
GODDESS
OF GOTHAM

"Manhattan Mystery Girl!" screamed the newspaper headlines.

New York is full of thirteen-year-old girls who think they're goddesses. But Kumari is the real deal. And she doesn't have a clue how she got there.

Kumari is a goddess-in-training who lives in a secret valley kingdom. She is destined to stay young forever, unlike people in the World Beyond. But Kumari longs to break out of her claustrophobic life at the Palace, where her only real friend is a baby vulture, and there's nothing to think about – except the mystery of her mother's death.

It's hard to kill a goddess, but someone did. And so Kumari steals away to the Holy Mountain, determined to summon Mamma back from the dead and to find out the truth.

But the next thing Kumari knows, she's in New York. Surrounded by strange buildings and even stranger people, and running for her life . . .

"A magnificent debut full of wit and humour "
Lovereading4kids

ISBN: 978 1 85340 956 1

Discover more about
The Island That Wasn't There
at:

www.piccadillypress.co.uk

☆ The latest news on forthcoming books

☆ Chapter previews

☆ Author biographies

☆ Fun quizzes

☆ Reader reviews

☆ Competitions and fab prizes

☆ Book features and cool downloads

☆ And much, much more . . .

Log on and check it out!

Piccadilly Press